Praise for *Hook Man Speaks*

"Knowing that this wonderful and affecting book is the only novel we shall ever have from Matt Clark is heartbreaking, but it's the kind of heartbreak we're grateful for."

—ELIZABETH GILBERT

"Matt Clark has concocted a story that's part picaresque, part urban folklore, part bildungsroman, and like no other novel I've ever read. The confidences of the specter who haunts lovers' lanes offer amazing surprises—a love affair with the Kentucky Fried lady, an employee discount at a funeral home, a Rosetta log. Just as surprising is the emotional and intellectual depth Clark gives to his characters and their bizarre situations."

—JOSH RUSSELL

"Matt Clark attempted to hold on to the uncontainable world by memorizing it, listing it, surveying it, savoring it, while satirizing and loving it. . . . It's hard not to see in the embrace and naming of so much of the anonymous but real world, an attempt to hold on to it and a premonition, perhaps, that it was not possible."

—ANDREI CODRESCU

HOOK | MAN | SPEAKS

MATT CLARK

𝕭
BERKLEY BOOKS, NEW YORK

B

A Berkley Book
Published by The Berkley Publishing Group
A division of Penguin Putnam Inc.
375 Hudson Street
New York, New York 10014

Copyright © 2001 by The Estate of Matthew Clark
Book design by Tiffany Kukec
Cover design by Erika Fusari
Cover illustration by Tsukushi

PRINTING HISTORY
Berkley trade paperback edition / October 2001

Visit our website at
www.penguinputnam.com

Library of Congress Cataloging-in-Publication Data

Clark, Matt, 1966–1998.
Hook Man speaks / Matt Clark.—Berkley trade pbk. ed.
p. cm.
ISBN 0-425-18162-6
I. Title.
PS3553.L28734 H66 2001
813'.54—dc21   2001025810

PRINTED IN THE UNITED STATES OF AMERICA

10 9 8 7 6 5 4 3 2 1

*I no longer love her, that's certain, but maybe I love
    her.*
Love is so short, forgetting is so long.

—PABLO NERUDA

*I think I ought to inform the reader that there has
just been a long interval.*

—VLADIMIR NABOKOV

HOOK | MAN | SPEAKS

PART | ONE

Most dreaded nightmare. Specter haunting campfires, slumber parties, freshman floors, treehouses. Supreme boogeyman. Me. *The Hook. Alive. Semi-whole. Contemplating my place in culture and history.*

   Boo.

"Do you ever recall being on Old County Line Road not far outside of Decatur, Georgia?" Dr. Brautigan says, Mont Blanc twitching above his yellow legal pad.

"Was it raining? Lots of lightning? Scary shadows?"

The good doctor consults his notes. "Um. Yes."

I weigh the facts. "I'm not positive," I say, "but I think so."

He lowers his pen, scratches the paper with it. "How about the River Road, south of Baton Rouge, Louisiana, 1972?"

"Hurricane weather? Smell of roadkill? Levee to the left of me, moo-cows to the right?"

Note checking. "I'm not sure," Dr. Brautigan says.

"Me, either."

"Think," Brautigan urges. "Think hard."

And I try. I really do. But all I can find in my mind is the inside of my mailbox. All is blackness. I can't see, can't tell if there's anything there waiting for me to come home and drag it out into the sunlight. I smell and smell, hoping for a trace of Rosemary's perfume. Is that it? Hovering over the doom-sweetened scent of just-mowed grass? I can't tell.

"I can't," I say out loud. I get up and leave the room without a good-bye, sprint from the building, don't stop until I'm at my front door, at my mailbox, heart pounding, hopeful, flinging open the tiny tin door, pawing inside, dragging out a Piggly Wiggly flyer (Whole Fryers 98 Cents!), VISA application, carpet-cleaning ad. That's it.

My spirits crash around my chigger-bit ankles.

It is forever until the mail carrier's next approach.

At our next session Dr. Brautigan says, "The Dan Dee Cabins, Ruidoso, New Mexico. Fall of 1969?"

I don't recall ever having been in New Mexico, but I almost say yes. I want badly to help Dr. Brautigan; he's been so terribly nice. "The very air smelled of thunder and tequila?" I venture.

"It did?" Dr. Brautigan says, jotting, nodding, smiling.

Dr. Brautigan is a folklorist at the University, engaged in an intensive study of me. For the last twenty-five years he's collected Hook Man stories from all over North America. Several months ago an article in *Harper's* prompted me to contact him. "I remember the sound of coyotes, possibly wild dogs," I tell him. "A gila monster had just bitten me on the toe, so I was really quite insane."

In addition to myriad psychological profiles, Dr. Brautigan is trying to ascertain how many times I actually struck, in light of how many unjustified reports exist about my exploits. "Now," Dr. Brautigan says, "the young woman—a Miss Lorena Hidalgo—says she saw you in the rearview mirror over her boyfriend's shoulder."

"Ah, yes," I say, and I actually feel for a moment that I truly might be recalling this, "I never got close to the car. The young woman squealed, and they drove off in their—was it a Camaro?"

"Mustang," Dr. Brautigan corrects.

"Red," I pronounce.

Brautigan checks his notes. "It doesn't say."

"The color of poppies," I continue.

"Like in *The Wizard of Oz*," Dr. Brautigan says.

"Devastatingly red," I say, even though I remember the poppies in Oz being orange. Orange poppies, blue gingham dress, white snow. In the distance, emerald towers. Overhead, broom-spun terror.

"So this is *not* a case in which you lost your hook in the door handle?"

"No. The hook was only detached forcibly once. And that was at a root-beer stand, actually."

"Fascinating," Brautigan says. "Tell me all about it."

I subscribe to these magazines: *Newsweek. GQ. Harper's*, as I have already pointed out. *Southern Living*, for the recipes. *The New Yorker. Mad. Men's Fitness. Southwest Review. Architectural Digest. Premiere. The Southern Review. The Atlantic Monthly. Esquire. Spy. The Nose. Rolling Stone. Vanity Fair*. I was a *Time* subscriber until their last format change. (You will notice: No *People*. No *Us*. No *Reader's Digest*.)

When Dr. Brautigan moved me to the University from Tallahassee, I called all the subscription departments to make them aware of my new address. Although each said it would not be a problem, the March issues of *Esquire* and *Southern Living* have never found their way to me. I am currently composing stinging letters of complaint.

When I first met Rosemary she impressed me by immediately asking what had become of my hand. We were sitting on neighboring stools at a café in Wichita Falls, Texas. "What happened?" she said.

"To me?" I was unused to such honest curiosity. In general, people ignore my hook completely. In general, people—excepting certain children and, of course, my "victims"—ignore ME completely.

"To your hand." She reached out and touched my hook. It was not, by most standards, a special touch. It was not slow and charged with erotic intention, nor tentative, like that of a frightened schoolgirl dared to touch a newly captured garden snake. Rosemary's touch was remarkable only in its normalcy, being no more aggressive than that of a grandmother reaching out to test the ripeness of a grocery store tomato.

It shocked me.

"I lost it," I told her, blushing.

She stared at me, waiting for an explanation.

"It was an accident."

"I should hope so," Rosemary said, turning back to her scrambled eggs.

"And you are how old?" Dr. Brautigan asked during our first session.

"I'm not sure," I said, smirking.

Brautigan didn't write anything down. He sat, staring at me, pen held cigarlike between his lips.

I gave him the *Miracle on 34th Street* answer: "As old as my tongue and a little older than my teeth." I smiled—showed him my perfect set of teeth—but Brautigan continued to just sit. People do this with me quite a bit. They assume I am leaving things out, that my incompleteness isn't just physical but verbal, possibly even mental.

Brautigan came at me from another direction. "What," he asked, "do you remember most vividly from your childhood?"

I remember saying, "I remember . . ."

When I was in fourth grade, my family moved to a farm near Alvarado, Texas. That was the year we studied dinosaurs, and were urged to search out fossils in our afternoon wanderings, ordered to present our finds to the class for examination and identification.

One day, rambling through a rocky cow pasture, I came upon a number of heart-shaped rocks, each stamped with an elaborate and beautiful design. The best ones I gathered carefully, cautious of the melon-yellow scorpions that were so plentiful—sometimes even in our bathtub—in the early fall. Selecting the three most perfect specimens, each a chalky-gray, fist-sized miracle, I carried them home to delicately bathe and dry them, wrapped each in a bed of toilet paper and set them next to my completed homework.

At school I presented the fossils with pride, announcing that I had found a veritable elephants' graveyard of hearts. A valentine quarry. But my discovery was not nearly so romantic or awesome as I had hoped it might be. The foundations of science did *not* quake.

"They're sea urchins," Mrs. Custer told me and the rest of the class. "From when this whole area was covered by an ocean millions of years ago. Not hearts. Just sea urchins. Common in virtually every area of North America," she concluded.

At that point in time, I was still whole. I ate my meals with two hands. Rode a bike like a normal boy. Played outfield, dreading the approach of any fly ball that might take me away from my contemplation of the turf and rocks and sprouting bluebonnets. When Mrs. Custer came to stand in front of me, I blushed and held both hands out, cupped to receive not a communion wafer but the shower of petrified sea urchins that tumbled from my teacher's upended palms.

Brautigan passes out questionnaires in his freshman survey class. From these, he determines the local spots most likely to harbor high school students' most ardent bursts of backseat passion. Of the forty-two students who complete the form, thirty-six are from Alpine or the surrounding area. Of those thirty-six, twenty-nine agree Indian Lodge State Park is a hotbed of hormonal tension and release. Twenty of those twenty-nine admit to losing their virginity there. Sixteen of those twenty are male. Seven of those sixteen are named Mike.

"Have you ever been?"

I have not, and I tell the doctor this.

"Would you like to go? That is, do you feel the desire to visit the area for your usual purpose?"

It's been a while since my last activity. I've almost entirely lost the urge. I shut my eyes and try to awaken the memory inside me. The darkness. The moonlit bumpers. Interiors lit by radio dials. Crickets. Branches breaking under my creeping step. Sepulchral organ chords that only I can hear.

"Well," I say, "I don't . . ."

But then I get an idea.

This is the first time I've seen Dr. Brautigan not wearing chinos, a denim shirt, beautiful silk tie. Instead, he sports jeans, my favorite flannel shirt (dollar-bill green and black with a few threads of red mixed in). He crouches in the bushes next to me. We've been here since dusk, sitting on our haunches, watching the skies darken, the ocotillo turn into hydras, the saguaro into Martians. I am just about to ask Dr. B. what he thinks about *The New Yorker*'s new image—its new smell—when I hear the murmur of an approaching vehicle. The murmur turns into a growl. Headlights sweeping past us like dragon eyes, a pickup truck rolls to a stop under a live oak twenty yards away.

"What if it's a drug drop-off?" Dr. Brautigan says.

"Shhh." The pickup's windows are down. An Eagles song wafts out to us. I give Brautigan the thumbs-up.

We wait.

"Don't watch," I whisper to Dr. Brautigan when I notice he is straining to see inside the truck. "That's not the point."

He nods.

Take It Easy.

Witchy Woman.

Lyin' Eyes.

Already Gone.

Desperado. I nudge Brautigan. "OK. Do it." Before he creeps out of the brush, I take off my hook and hand it to him. "You'll need this," I say.

As if he were in a cartoon, he gulps audibly. Takes the hook, grips it in his right hand, pulls the cuff of his sleeve down around it. "Good man," I hiss.

Hunkered close to the ground, lurching like an ape, he moves toward the pickup. I try to send a psychic command to him. *"Limp!"* I think. He either gets the message or remembers how we rehearsed this, because he pauses for a moment, shakes his head, then proceeds, dragging one leg like dead weight. I get a shiver watching Brautigan do this. It's like watching myself. A memory. But in 3-D. Tangible.

He's close to the pickup, only a few feet behind the tailgate. My heart races, claws its way up my rib cage into my esophagus, where it cowers behind my uvula, watching, waiting for the inevitable scream.

Brautigan inches to the target, carefully reaches out toward the door handle and . . .

. . . drops the hook. It hits the ground with a dull clang.

Brautigan stiffens. Waits to be caught. But nothing happens. Turning to look at me, he shrugs, holds his palms out like, "Now what?" I return the gesture. He reaches down slowly and gets the hook, then scurries back to where I'm crouching, my mouth agape.

"I can't do it," he says in a normal voice.

I clamp my hand—my good hand—over his mouth.

"What was that?" the girl in the pickup gasps, coming up for air.

"What?"

"I thought I heard something. Somebody talking."

"Nah," her date brays.

"Yes. I'm sure."

They argue for a few moments. Then he starts the pickup—you can hear his frustration in the growl and roar of the engine—and they speed away.

Brautigan relaxes. Sits back in the leaves. "Wow," he says. "So that's what it's like."

"No," I contend. "That's what it's *sort* of like. *If* they tell their friends what happened, the mysterious sound will be attributed to a mountain lion. A lost Pomeranian, maybe."

"A Pomeranian?" Brautigan says, disappointed.

"Possibly rabbits."

"Rabbits?"

"Bunnies," I elucidate.

"How embarrassing," Brautigan murmurs.

"Hey," I say. "It's my reputation at stake."

*   *   *

I arrived in Alpine by train. Dr. Brautigan sent me enough money to travel by air, but I chose to ride the rails, to see the land, all the crossings with their flashing lights and zebra-striped arms. I sold all my possessions in a garage sale that—even though it wasn't much— seemed to thrill the college students and old ladies who milled around my cast-off clothes and books and mementos. I suspect they were excited mainly because everything I owned had originally been bought from garage sales. I occupied a home composed entirely of refuse from Tallahassee's spring cleanings. My yard became a clearinghouse of thrift and kitsch for the most discriminating.

My bamboo couch and end table and bowling trophies (not really mine) and Fiesta ware and all of it—*all of it*—went and went fast. I had lettered my signs FRIDAY SATURDAY AND SUNDAY ONLY, but on Saturday morning there was so little left that I decided it wasn't worth setting up the tables to display the measly leftovers. Nevertheless, by 9:30 A.M. a horde of eager shoppers clamored at my doorstep.

"Open up," they demanded.

"It's all gone," I said through the screen door.

"Impossible," one man said.

A woman who was probably his wife honked, "What're you, holding something back?"

"I'm looking for salt and pepper shakers," an old woman at the rear of the crowd crooned. "In funny shapes. Do you have any of those?"

"It's all gone," I repeated. "Yesterday was a sellout."

The crowd quieted, but began to edge closer to the porch. I grabbed a box half full of forks missing tines and matchless socks and set it outside the door. "There," I said. "You can have it."

A representative of the group advanced and dug through the box. "Trash," he said to the people behind him. He looked up at me and, shaking his head, hissed, "Trash."

Once again the mass of people began to crowd the porch. "You give us trash?" the salt-shaker lady squeaked.

"Stop!" I commanded. "Stop right there." They did. "That's it. That's everything I have. Now go away." I raised my hook next to my face. "Before something bad happens." I drove my hook through the flimsy screen and ripped it from top to bottom.

Screaming, the shoppers fled, leaving me to finish packing, positive my security deposit was now forever lost. But happy to be rid of my earthly possessions. And with a pocket full of cold, hard cash earmarked for the train-station newsstand, a tabloid utopia.

A train affords so much to its passengers, so much more than airplanes do. The comfort is superior: Legroom. Food. The absence of sickening turbulence. No attendants who hate you but are unable to speak their minds. No fluctuating air pressure, ear popping, head aching. Trains allow one to revel in the passage of time and trees and cities and magazines. On a train, I can wallow in magazines, piglike, rooting out truffles of well-researched health articles, stylish photo essays, revealing profiles and delicious short stories. There are treasures to be found

in periodicals, but one must search carefully, without haste. On a train,
I can hunt lazily and savor my finds languorously.

"What a mess of magazines," the woman sitting to my right said
in the middle of a bridge. "What are you? Rich?"

"No," I explained. "I had a garage sale."

"A garage sale? Oh, I love garage sales."

"Me, too," interjected the woman on the other side of her.

"You can find the most incredible bargains. On priceless items
sometimes."

"How was your garage sale?" the first woman asked.

"A sellout."

"Yes," she said. "But how was it? Did you put your wares on the
front porch, back porch, sidewalk, driveway?"

"Or did you actually have it in your garage? Maybe your carport?"

"Carport garage sales are nice."

"A little shade."

"In case of rain."

"Or a day too bright to see through."

I broke in. "It was just in my front yard."

"Oh, a yard sale. Well, that's really quite different. In subtle ways."

"You advertised?" the first woman asked.

"Of course he did!"

"But how, exactly?"

"In the paper?"

"More likely just signs around the neighborhood. Hand-lettered,
or printed by one of those Quick-Sign places?"

"You can get them at hardware stores, too. Signs. About garage sales and vicious dogs and solicitors."

"Too bland, though, those. Too generic."

"But recognizable. Easily spotted on telephone poles. Pros know the signs."

"Word of mouth. That's a fine way to promote yourself, don't forget."

"I," I said, "made signs and put them up around the neighborhood."

"But no newspaper advertisements? Quite a risk you took, Mister. The media is a powerful tool. You ought to know that."

"My niece's boyfriend once bought a Porsche through the paper."

"You can find it all in the paper."

"He paid bottom dollar for it."

"People advertise to sell. That's the point."

"Car was worth fifty thousand. He got it for five hundred."

"He did not."

"Did. Answered an ad. Went to the address. Woman sold him the car for five hundred. Perfect condition. Low mileage. Practically new."

"What luck."

"Woman told him her husband had run off to Mexico with his secretary. Phoned from Acapulco and told her to sell the car and send him the cash. Everything else was hers."

"The cad!"

"So she sold the car. For *five hundred dollars*."

"Serves him right."

"Wonderful car. Drives like a dream, my niece says. Like a dream."

"My dentist bought a Ferrari once. Cheap. Got it from a used-car dealer."

"My brother-in-law sells cars. New. Not used."

"Just as much money in used."

"No doubt."

"Can't live without a car these days. And if you're a dentist, you can afford a nice car. But my dentist got this Ferrari cheap."

"Saved a bundle, did he?"

"Thought he did. But the truth of the matter is, he sold the car right back to the used-car lot."

"Didn't like the car?"

"*Loved* the car. From a distance. Inside it smelled like rotten meat."

"You don't say."

"Tragic. He took the car back, and the salesman told him the car just wouldn't stay sold. He kept lowering the price, and people kept buying the car and bringing it back. Man *died* in it."

"My word."

"Wasn't found for days." She paused, lowered her voice. "Summertime."

"My word!"

"Late July."

"Horrible."

"Too terrible for words."

"I hate to think of it."

"Car's still there," the woman said to me. "Man with a wad of cash and a strong stomach might could tame her. You ought to look into it."

"I'm afraid my sense of smell is very sensitive," I said.

The women both noticed my hook. One looked away. "Only natural," the other one said. "Mother Nature takes care of her children. The Good Lord provides. Stevie Wonder can play the piano like an angel. Blind as a bat and he plays like an angel."

"I'm not especially musical," I offered.

"It's never too late to learn," she said.

"A student told me about this," Brautigan says.

We're driving away from town, south, past the abandoned Rock Shop, past creaking University Stadium. Alpine falls behind us like a toy on a sandbox hill, Fisher-Price village, Lilliputian college-ville. Midget post office, five-and-dime, movie theater, barbecue joint, halls of learning, all of them shrinking behind me until they are gone. (Or maybe I'm getting larger, like a fifties monster-movie radiation victim grown to dwarf loved ones and enemies, finally falling dead amongst a mob of olive-green tanks and colossal-boot-flattened bazooka shooters.) The city evaporates. Ahead of us, sunburnt mesas glow red in the waning daylight, monsters bigger even than myself.

"How come you've never invited me to your class?" I ask.

"What? Class? Why would you want to do that?"

"You could introduce me. As an artifact or witness or text. Something."

Brautigan shakes his head. "We'll see," he says, then changes the subject. "This particular phenomenon is not uncommon. I've read a number of reports placing it in almost every midwestern state. Big in

Missouri for some reason. But I had no idea it was *here* until this student told me about it." Brautigan steers with his left hand on the wheel, right resting on the stick shift, comfortable, at ease, relaxed, like it feels good to drive that way.

"I like it," I mumble.

"What? The Volkswagen? Thanks. Had it forever."

"My father, he *really* would have liked it."

"Ah, yes, wind in his hair," Brautigan acknowledges. "The open road."

We roll over a snake warming itself on the asphalt.

"Ooops," Brautigan grunts.

I turn around quickly to see if the snake has survived or if it lies segmented and writhing, hopeless. But the road behind us is empty; the snake has either hightailed it onto the shoulder to take inventory of its squashed parts and curse us, or it's hanging on to the bumper even now, slithering up over the downed ragtop, tongue-flicking, spine-sore, hungry for revenge.

"They don't completely die until sunset," Brautigan says. "Snakes."

"It is sunset," I remind him. "And that's not really true. That's a myth."

"Really?"

"Really."

The car slows to a stop. "I guess," Brautigan conjectures, "this is it."

We're parked in front of a railroad crossing. There is no flashing light or jerkily lowering arm. Just identifying X signs on either side of the road. The landscape is so unencumbered by anything you'd have to be blind and deaf to miss a train bulleting through the desert here. On top of that, this road is spectacularly lonesome. I suspect it peters out no more than a mile or two ahead, the black tar and weather-cracked cement dissipating into sand, hardscrabble and the occasional Apache arrowhead. "Iron Horse," I say.

"What? Oh, yes. Well. Here we are."

"So now what?"

Brautigan gives the car a punch of gas, rolling us up onto the slight rise where road and rails mesh. "We pull up here like so, turn the motor off"—he does—"and wait for the dead kids to push us off the tracks to safety." He reaches behind my seat and begins to rummage around. I can hear a slight splash of water, ice against glass, glass against glass, glass and ice and water against Styrofoam, skin against glass, water against water. "I have been told some level of intoxication is advantageous in conjuring them." He pulls his arm back into the front seat holding two beers. "Drink 'em if you got 'em."

The cooling engine clicks and creaks, groans, settles, hisses. It's dark out. The cloudy sky shields us from the stars and whatever moon is up at bat. When my eyes finally adjust to the headlights' absence, the road ahead becomes almost visible. A jackrabbit, its fur vaguely luminous, plops onto the center stripe, stops, sits up on its hind legs to sniff the air.

"Ah, peace at last." Brautigan sighs, taking a long pull on his beer. "Kids're having a sleepover at the house tonight. It'll be crank calls, water balloons and Ouija board hysteria till two at least."

"What dead children?" I ask.

"What?"

"What dead children? Will push us to safety?"

Brautigan nods and belches. "Oh, the ones from the school bus that got stuck on the track when the train was coming and couldn't stop in time. They push us to safety. The ghosts, that is."

"Wow," I say.

"Well, in reality it's just the tilt of the road. It looks like we're sitting on perfectly level ground here, but that's an illusion. We're imperceptibly rolling right now. Eventually we'll gain momentum and roll on over to the other side. Saved."

"How do you know we're not on level ground?"

"Good point," Brautigan admits. "I brought a carpenter's thingy. We'll get out afterwards and do some measuring. When we look for the fingerprints."

"What fingerprints?"

"The kids' fingerprints. That's the best part, and a fairly recent development in this particular activity. After we're safely across we get out and—according to legend—find dozens of little fingerprints all over the trunk and bumper."

I think about the snake we ran over and wonder if he's anticipated our mission and is coiled patiently, nuzzled up against the license plate, waiting for us to investigate our mysterious source of motion. "Creepy," I say.

"You betcha. Another beer?"

I gulp the last of my first before accepting another. We take turns gulping and wiping at our mouths with the backs of our hands, careful not to move in unison, fighting the rhythm our car-bound union nudges us toward.

"I feel like we're waiting for me to show up," I say.

"What? Huh?"

"Like we're waiting for the Hook Man to come get us," I clarify.

"Oh. Yeah. Scary. Yikes! You're in the car with me!" Brautigan laughs. "Ever take on a convertible before?" he asks.

I think back through the sundry vehicles in my history, the quarterbacks' nifty Firebirds (black with gold trim), the borrowed family wagons (baby seat strapped in the back), ailing Plymouths, Suburbans, Impalas, souped-up, customized farm trucks, Fieros (ripe to crash and burn), Mustangs (always red), ridiculous Gremlins, Corvairs, Pintos, stout Broncos, Jeep Cherokees, Chevy Blazers, fathers' AWOL Oldsmobiles, Lincolns, Cadillacs, Volvos, Audis, drug-money Jaguars, hand-me-down Skylarks, thoughtless Corvettes, Thunderbirds, Chevettes, sick-making Good Times Vans. "No convertibles come to mind," I tell the doctor.

"Really? Yes. Well, they're probably difficult to approach correctly. You'd risk observation before the ultimate moment."

Silence again.

"How many children are there?"

"I've got two boys and a girl," Brautigan answers.

"No. The ghosts. How many are there supposed to be?"

"Good question," Brautigan says. "I don't know for sure. Some research might be done on that. 'How many children would your average Joe expect to die in a school bus/railroad crossing tragedy? How many baby ghosts does it take to make a good story?' "

"What are their names?"

"The ghosts?"

"Your kids."

"Oh. Oldest is Kyle. Next is Amelia. Then Thad. It's Kyle's sleepover, so—"

I hold my hand up to stop Brautigan from saying anything more. We're rolling. I can feel it. After Brautigan's voice stops, I can hear the tires humming, crunching gravel against the road. The speed we attain is unmeasurable in terms of miles per hour: faster than a snail, slower than a fire ant. A couple of yards beyond the tracks, we settle to a stop.

"I'll be damned," Brautigan says. He reaches beneath his seat and pulls forth a carpenter's level, then a flashlight. "Let's check it out," he suggests, sounding more Hardy Boy–esque than professorial.

We get out and walk back to the tracks. Brautigan crouches with the level, sets it down; then he's on his stomach next to it, eyeing the bubble of air trapped and searching for an escape. "Oh, it's there all right. Just barely there, but there." He gathers himself and stands, turns the flashlight up under his chin, throwing shadows onto his face. "Gravity's a bunch of ghosts," he says Karloffishly.

I'm considering the back of the car from a foot or two away, examining for snakes and fingerprints. Brautigan's flashlight beam clarifies. "Nothing," I say.

"You sound disappointed," Brautigan snorts.

"I feel like the Easter Bunny at a court-martial."

"I didn't get that."

"You don't believe in me," I moan.

Brautigan is flabbergasted. "Come again?"

"I watched you get off debunking a pretty nifty story that sounded perfectly plausible to me. Am I next? What kind of hardware will it take to exorcise me from your office into the vault of silly legerdemain? Will you tape-measure my conscience, then hacksaw my ego and sand down my id?"

We stand a long time then. Not talking. Me breathing hard. Brautigan's mouth agape. We're a weird tableau hinted at, then revealed by, then bathed in and dazzled with the headlights of an approaching car. Out a sunroof a boy's voice snipes, "Hey! Quit hogging the dead kids. Give somebody else a chance."

I check my mail and find a lone postcard. From someone named Rusty to someone named DeeDee Eastep, who this person named Rusty believes for some reason is living at my address. This is not true. I have never heard of DeeDee Eastep. Not even from neighbors who have related to me the recent and distant history of my abode. Uncle Sam forgive me, I will keep the postcard—it shows a beach and a sunset and a sailboat—and I will pretend that it is addressed to me and signed, *Love, Rosemary*. I will invent a message better than the one Rusty wrote to DeeDee, except I will leave the last line alone. It reads, "See you soon."

On Halloween I dress up like a pirate. Children approach my door holding out bags bursting with Milky Ways, Snickers and Pixie Stix. Candy corn, Baby Ruths, Twizzlers and Three Musketeers. Circus Peanuts, Red Hots, ChocoLotta Crunchies, Milk Duds, Raisinets, Jujubes, Butterfingers, Sticky-Lickums, Cherry Bomms, Blow Pops, Sugar Daddies, WhamZ!, Good-n-Plenty, Spittoonz, Yummy-Mummies, Monkey-Doodles, Bytz-o-Hades, Watermelon Yeehaws, Woolly-Booger Sugar Sticks, Goopyloopies, Mount Caramels, Tootsie Rolls, Big Fat Logs, Gooey-Goony Moon Fruities, Frog Boogers, Newtonian Apple-Bombs, Slug-Bumpies, LavaLumpos, Butternutty Yumdumz, Slimy-limey Leper Tongues. Bubble Gum. They're supposed to bellow, "Trick or treat!" but many of them swallow their voices when they see my hook. Even other pirates are intimidated. Their timbers shiver.

"Oh, don't be silly," mothers coo. "It's only a costume!" They push their children toward the bowl of SweeTARTS I hold out, cupped by my good hand and brightly polished hook.

"Trick or treat," they gasp, before grabbing a handful and scrambling away.

They know. Somehow, they know.

At a little before ten, the doorbell rings yet again. I'm almost out of candy, but the torrent of clowns and skeletons has diminished to a wee trickle of older children, some of them students from the University, belching laughter and asking for beers. I put down my *Esquire* and go to the door.

"Trick or treat," Dr. Brautigan says. He's dressed like me. Like *me*. Not like a pirate. Like the Hook Man. He even has a hook, which he holds up to show me. "I didn't think you'd be home," he says. "I thought you might be out. Somewhere. Doing something."

"I've just been reading," I tell him. "Would you like to come in?"

Brautigan stoops down to examine my jack-o-lantern's crossed eyes and goofy teeth. "Nice," he observes. "No. No, thanks. I just dropped by to say Happy Halloween." He stands up and shakes his head. "I was positive you'd be gone."

"Well," I say, "here I am."

"I just thought maybe this was sort of a special day for you."

It hits me what Brautigan is getting at, and I take a step back. "You thought I'd be out doing what? Scaring people? Skulking in bushes? Leaping out at toddlers?"

Brautigan looks at his shoes, ashamed.

"Is that what—is that what *you've* been doing?"

"No!" Brautigan insists. "Not really. I've been handing out candy at home. Just like you."

I sigh and turn around to go back inside. I'm right in the middle of an unbearable Jay McInerney story. I swear, *Esquire* would publish his canceled checks. "I'll see you tomorrow, Doctor," I say. "Happy Halloween."

"And some nights," I whispered to my brother, my voice rising to bounce off our ceiling and back down to his bottom bunk, "some nights, nights when the moon is full, I hear it."

"You do?" he said, near tears.

"Against the screen. Scratching against the window screen. You've never heard that?"

"It's just a branch," my brother said. "Or a bug."

"No," I contended, "it's my hand. It clawed its way up through the earth, past all the rocks and worms and around the little tombstone, and it's come to find me."

"They didn't bury it, though, did they?" my brother argued. "I thought the hospital did something with it?"

"They threw it out with the trash," I explained. "And I went and dug through all the shit and bloody sheets until I found it. And I took it. And I buried it."

"Where?" my brother gasped.

"If I show you or tell you, it might come looking for you," I said. Silence.

"I don't think any of that's true," my brother insisted.

"Believe whatever you like," I told him. "But look out the window. The moon is full. And there's not a lick of breeze. If you hear anything scratching against the window tonight, it's no branch. No bug. So lay very still. Be very quiet. And hope that it doesn't get in."

Dr. Brautigan meets me at the door of his office holding a bottle of cognac with a black ribbon around its neck. "I am so sorry," he says. "Really. My behavior was offensive. I realize that and hope you will accept this and my apology."

"No problem," I say. I take the bottle and measure its heft in my good hand. "Thanks. I like cognac."

"Are you Catholic?" Brautigan says.

The non sequitur confuses me. "Well, yes. I am a little. That is to say, I was brought up Catholic."

"Because today's a holy day, right? A feast of some kind?"

"Something like that. I'm afraid to say—well, I guess I'm actually a little ashamed to say I've forgotten."

The last time I went to confession I knelt outside the confessional and looked at the way people's fingerprints could be seen on and around the handle. On the frame of the door there was a whole palm print pressed ghostlike onto the wood. I was the only one waiting a turn. Without thinking I reached up with my hook and made the tiniest scratch in the middle of the palm. "Just a moment," the priest inside the booth said. Finally a young woman—mascara Niagara'd chin-ward—came out, and I crept inside to hunker behind the mysterious screen.

I confessed everything but the scratch on the confessional. That wasn't a sin to me, but a signature, like all those fingerprints, all those whorls of flesh and oil and dirt. The scratch was the sound of my one hand clapping.

I finally bring the subject up myself. "Why," I ask Dr. Brautigan, "have you never asked me about my hook?"

"About your hook?" He sounds startled. "That's all we've talked about for months now."

"No. I mean, you've never asked me how I got my hook. You've never asked me how it came to be that I *am* the Hook Man."

"Oh," Dr. Brautigan says. "I guess I've been a little reluctant to broach that subject. Afraid the memory might be too painful."

"That's funny," I tell Brautigan, "because it didn't hurt at all." It was sore afterward, of course, despite all the painkillers. But when it happened, I felt nothing.

*   *   *

Rosemary lived in a little house just behind the Wichita Falls Drive-In. We couldn't see the movies from there, of course. They didn't seep through the heavy wooden screen. And because the car speakers were so small, we never heard the soundtracks, either. But the laughter. *That* we heard. And the screams. We could sit out on her back porch, and the back of the screen towered above us, part billboard, part plywood roller coaster. The light from the projector leaked around the edges, giving the whole affair a shimmering corona. It was weird and beautiful and exciting to be sitting out there listening to the bullbats squeak, waiting for people to ha-ha all at once on account of some poor sap getting a pie in the face, or yelp and squeal when the spaceships landed and let loose with a barrage of ray-guns. Rosemary had a big metal porch glider that always seemed cool, as if just taken from a freezer. She'd sit, and I'd lay my head on her lap so she could stroke my hair with her slow-moving nails while we eavesdropped on the drive-in patrons.

That's what we were doing the night she told me who she really was.

"I'm the Kentucky Fried Rat Lady," she said out of the blue. We hadn't been talking at all. She just blurted it out.

Uncertain, I held my tongue. The way my head was turned, I couldn't see her face. In a car hidden by the colossal screen a girl screamed, then laughed like a donkey braying.

"I mean, I am *the* Kentucky Fried Rat Lady. The one you've heard about."

Long pause.

"I'm not sure I've heard about you," I confessed.

"Oh, you know. The lady who took her family to eat at Kentucky Fried Chicken and ended up taking a bite out of a rat that had fallen into the batter and been deep-fried."

I waited a beat or two. "So you're her," I said, even though I'd never heard that tale before. "I didn't know you had a family." With my ear pressed against her thigh, I listened to my heart beating wildly. "Do you have a family?"

"Well," she said, "the story has been perverted a little bit. The truth is, I've got diabetes. And I lose feeling in my extremities, my hands and my feet sometimes. And I was sitting right here one summer day eating fried chicken with my shoes off. And I fell asleep."

She paused. "I see," I said.

"There's more. The chicken fell down on the porch and a bunch of rats—from the drive-in, I imagine—came over and ate the chicken, and then ate my feet. My feet were right there by the chicken. *They* didn't know the difference. And *I* couldn't feel them chowing down. So when I woke up, they'd devoured my toes and the balls of my feet and my soles and my heels. Gone, gone, gone. I was completely without feet. Still am, for that matter. Story made the papers, as you would probably guess, but people took the story and made it a little less gruesome—or a little more gruesome, depending on how often you eat out—than it already was. Making me the Kentucky Fried Rat Lady."

"Sort of like I'm the Hook Man."

"A little like that," Rosemary said.

"I've been written up," she continued, "in journals and magazines.

All kinds of places. Not the real story. The fake one. According to these articles, I get punished in the story because I was too lazy to cook for my family. I'm supposed to serve as a warning to mothers. *Don't feed your kids fast food. Cook!*"

"So, do you have any kids?" I asked.

"Nope. Just a couple of fake feet."

"Weren't you angry?" Dr. Brautigan says.

"What makes you think I would get angry?"

"She seems to have waited quite a while before telling you she was herself not complete. She seems to have let you think for quite some time that you were the deformed one in your relationship."

"Who said anything about being deformed? Or not complete? Our relationship had nothing to do with existence in the physical plane. Our love was—is—cerebral. That's why I'd never noticed her feet were prosthetic. It never occurred to me to look."

Another postcard for DeeDee. This one shows a jellyfish sprawled on a pristine beach. The photographer stood just above the creature. Light hits its electric-blue body in such a way that it radiates an aura of magic, a shimmering halo of colors more appropriate for a Looney Tunes short than a stranded monster. Its long white tentacles, Tannenbaum-topping angel-hair, are arranged neatly, model-like. Above it and to the left, at the edge where a postal phantom has stamped a few red numbers, a tiny shell, perfect, unbroken, awaits the coming of a toddler's chubby digits. The shell and the jellyfish work together (good cop/bad cop, sweet and sour, beauty and the beautiful beast) to ensure each golden day at the shore includes a brush with pain and danger. Will the mother get there in time to thwart the jellyfish's stinging? Will the father have taught Baby the no-no's of beachcombing? Will the photographer stand there, like a wartime Pulitzer-hound, finger poised to press and catch the dreadful *ouch* and swelling flesh?

On the back of the postcard, the lovesick Rusty has scrawled above his signature a gawking eye, a bulging heart, a puffy sheep.

I tell Dr. Brautigan about my father, about how he worked on our farm and did maintenance at the Niblett Funeral Parlor in town. This extra job sounds a great deal more morbid than it actually was. The fact of the matter is, my father never—not once—set foot inside the Niblett Funeral Parlor. The entirety of his duties lay outside those quiet marble halls. (Oh, yes, *I do* know they were quiet. My father never went in, but I did.) My father kept the grass neat. He carefully edged the sidewalks and driveways. Polished the model tombstones—markers, they're called. He painted the shutters and detailed the discreet sign on a regular basis. Planted flowers in beds and pruned crepe myrtle trees into neat, vertical lines. Kept the hearse and black Cadillacs in good running condition, too. But he didn't go inside. This was part of his contract with Mr. Niblett. My father had a deep dislike, not for death or corpses or embalming fluid, but for coffins. He hated tight spaces period. Couldn't abide riding in cars that weren't convertibles.

Kept—much to my mother's dismay—all his clothes hanging out in his bedroom, fearful as he was of closets. Shirts on bedposts. Socks on a lampshade. Underwear slung across a picture of my mother's mother. Pants neatly folded over a ladderback chair. He insisted there always be at least one open window in any room he entered. So when he ran over my hand with the riding lawnmower one day—I was lolling in front of a marker, having just scrubbed out its engraved letters with an old toothbrush, pretending I was, as I was about to become, a victim of some horrible accident—he carried me only as far as the door to the Funeral Home. From there Mr. Niblett took me—made me walk on my own—into the embalming room, where I lay on a metal table waiting for the ambulance to show up. A radio was on full blast. Mr. Niblett was a Billie Holiday fan, and he whistled along with Lady Blue ("I Cover the Waterfront") while he wrapped my stump up good and tight and put a tourniquet around my arm. From the entrance, several rooms away, my father hollered, "Is he okay?"

Mr. Niblett was combing my hair, parting it on the wrong side. He wiped the sweat off my forehead with a little white towel. "Dandy," he called back. "You want to come in?"

"No. That's all right," my father said. "I'll just stay out here."

"Will they be able to sew it back on?" I asked Mr. Niblett.

He seemed surprised to hear me talk, as if he'd forgotten I was still alive, as if I was one of his usual customers. "Oh. Well, they might be able to. If it's not too chopped up."

"If they can't, will it get buried?"

Mr. Niblett smiled. "Thinking of that employee's discount, aren't you?"

*   *   *

Dr. Brautigan says, "So what was your relationship with your father like after the accident?"

"That sounds more like a therapist's question than a folklorist's."

Brautigan hums to himself for a moment. "Yes, well. I'm actually curious." He puts his pen down so that it balances on the pad, which is balancing on his knee. Clasping his hands in front of him, he says, "Did you ever talk about it? Did he apologize?"

"He died," I say.

Silence. "I'm sorry," Brautigan murmurs.

"He had a heart attack one day while walking the fenceline; we had some calves missing. When he didn't come in for supper, my mother sent my brother out to look for him," I explain. "The doctors say it happened very quickly, that he was in no pain. Which may be true, even though it seems that doctors always say that. 'This is going to hurt just a little bit. You won't feel a thing. He went without suffering.' "

"I'm sorry," Dr. Brautigan says again.

"It was a very bad summer for us," I conclude.

The worst occasion in the history of magazine publishing—the very nadir!—must be the invention of the perfume-strip insert. I've taken to tearing them out as soon as they arrive. In a box in the hall closet I've deposited every reeking one, anxious to know how many will ac-

cumulate in a year. Eternity, Passion, Opium, Joop, Polo, Poison, Dia-
mond, Idaho!, Montezuma, Aspen, Mr. Pierre, Black Scorpion, Grand
Teton, Flying Dutchman, Dominator, LMNOP, Stetson, Lola!, tsunami,
Spellbinder, Soliloquy, Atlas, Logjam, Caribou, Ludwig, Samba,
Mambo, Rhumba, Chatterley, Vladimir, Lava, Bliss, Torquemada,
Flint, Devil-May-Care, Whitewater, Winter Morning, Vernal, Equinox,
Mesa, Calliope, Grandstand, Olivia!, Hyacinth, Fascinating Rhythm,
Glacier, Canyon, Cousteau, Mantle, Antlers, Diva, Clover, Buddha, Sin-
fonia, L'Unacy, Sabre's Edge, Antigone, Misty Glade, Debauchery by
Flynn, Huntsman, Two O'Clock Phantom, Favorite Stranger, Cavalier,
Centripetal Force, Chanteuse, Gershwin, Tumbleweed Memories,
Voyeur, Shark, Vox, Zen, Yu, O!, Etc. I mean, etc., as in "and so on." I
have yet to see an ad for a cologne or perfume called Etc., but I have
faith in the industry. Every time I open the hall closet to deposit another strip into its fragrant cage, I am careful to cover my nose and
mouth. The fumes, I suspect, may well be mustard-gas deadly. Like
toxic waste or mercury, the perfume strips must be handled cautiously. As with an experimental strain of virus or a maniacal pachy-
derm, their captivity is of the utmost importance.

"You know something," Dr. Brautigan says, interrupting me, "I find it
very curious that you are so terribly interested in coming to my class.
It occurs to me that you've spent a large part of your existence lurking,
skulking, avoiding light and recognition. And now, suddenly, you want
to be introduced. You want to be showcased. You want to be in the
spotlight. I don't get it."

"So you don't want me to come to your class?" I ask.

"I want to know why you want to come to my class."

I think for a second. "I want," I say, "to see them. Their faces and baseball caps and Mickey Mouse watches, their manicured fingernails and expensive tennis shoes, their fraternity shirts and high school class rings and rat-packed purses. In the daylight. In a normal setting. I want to see them breathing regularly and thinking sensibly and taking notes."

"Few, if any of them, take notes," Brautigan says. "But is that really what you want? Couldn't you do that sitting on a bench near the library?"

"I want to see them still," I say. "Motionless. Like models posing for a sculptor."

"And what about you? Do you want them to see you?"

"I want to sit among them. I don't want to stand out from them. So, in answer to your question, yes and no. I want to be seen and not to be seen. At the same time."

Brautigan taps his pen against his teeth. "I don't know what to say," he says. "We'll see."

When I tell you I read every word of every magazine I get, I mean it. How else could you account for me finding this item tucked under the change-of-address information in the most recent *Texas Monthly*? "Subscribers preferring scent-free issues," the copy read, "may call 1-800-NOS-SAFE."

Did I call?

I did not. I'm not entirely sure why, but I didn't. I memorized the number, of course. (I doubt I'll ever forget it. How could I? I couldn't tell you the starting date of any war in recorded history, but I can recite a litany of noisome telephone "numbers.") Even as I reached for my phone's receiver, it occurred to me that I might be making a grave mistake. I shut my eyes and pictured myself opening my mailbox to find a *Gentleman's Quarterly* reeking of nothing more than that same mailbox's steely innards, or worse, my mail carrier's gratuitous Brut.

By necessity, I avoided my phone for the duration of the afternoon. 1-800-NOS-SAFE, indeed.

When Dr. Brautigan doesn't show up for our morning appointment, I think nothing of it. We all have mornings that go in directions we never anticipated or desired. I wait around his office for an hour and a half, leafing through folklore periodicals, trying to imagine the tunes that accompany the ballads transcribed therein: "Tom Dooley," "Mary McCree," "Hinkey Poteet," "The Blue Fire Coal Mine Murders," "Lucy the Serving Girl's Secret." Finally, I wander to the lecture hall where Brautigan's survey class meets, figuring he'll show up there, at least. Students drift in like dazed shipwreck survivors. I sit at the rear of the room, watching the boys kick back in their seats, boots up on the row in front of them. The girls laze about in groups of two and three, sighing and pouting and doodling in spiral notebooks. After ten minutes of waiting for Brautigan, they grow restless and begin to gauge each other's patience with blank stares, raised eyebrows. Eventually one brave youth in a denim jacket rolls out of his makeshift recliner and lumbers to the door. Without looking back he leaves. Slowly at first, then in a tide of grins and whistles, they all follow the first cowboy's lead.

His Pied Piper routine is capped by my own disappointed and un-witnessed exit.

At home, my answering machine blinks to let me know I've been away too long. "Dr. Brautigan here," the recorder reports. "I was wondering if maybe you could come down to the police station and help me clear up a little problem."

Dear Dr. Brautigan: (the letter I wrote in response to his article began)

I read with great excitement your recent piece in Harper's *regarding the antics of the "Hook Man" character. I found your prose style fresh and straightforward and your method of organization and presentation entertaining without being lackadaisical.*

It was with some concern, however, that I studied your observations on what sundry neuroses the Hook Man may possess that drive "him" to attack helpless lovebirds. You see—and I hope you will believe me when I tell you this is not *a joke—I am* the Hook Man *and am in no way whatsoever like the psychological profile you fabricated. For one thing, my sexual history is hardly bizarre. I have never been "involved" with any of*

the deviant types you list. Furthermore, my adolescent family
life was exceptionally normal and healthy. My mother and
brother can and will attest to that should you need corroborat-
ing witnesses.

Please do not think that I am chastising you for your mis-
takes. I am only trying to help you better understand your own
research. Indeed, I am flattered by your interest and would be
happy to help you in any way I can.

Sincerely,
Leonard Gage
(The Hook Man)

My money comes from the settlement with the lawnmower company,
of course. It wasn't much to begin with, and dwindles perilously,
wasted on a life of skulking and magazine perusal. But it lets me live,
if somewhat frugally, in a world of leisure. And when I need to bail a
friend out of jail, I can do so. Actually, Dr. Brautigan is the first friend
I've had reason to rescue from the calaboose. (I've known other
friends, certainly, but can count no criminals among their ranks.)

"Says you could explain," the detective mumbles, nodding at
where Brautigan sits slumped in a straight-backed chair, wearing his
Hook Man getup. The plastic hook, preserved in a see-through evidence bag, rests amid a collage of coffee-stained Styrofoam cups and
tattered sugar packets. "Says you could explain why it is we found him
loitering in the oleanders at City Park. Says he's a scientist or something."

"Professor," Dr. Brautigan corrects.

"Right. *Professor*. Says he's doing research." The detective notices my own hook and pauses. "That real?" he asks, gesturing.

"Genuine article," I admit, thumping the table so the cups and sugar packets and fake hook all bounce.

My first time.

It's a national, possibly universal obsession, firsts. The first man to do this. The first woman to do that. The first hog to swim the Mississippi. First dogcatcher to apprehend a zoo-wayward anaconda alone. Guinness has made a name for himself cataloguing firsts. People risk their lives and souls for his attention, for one line in his thick, ridiculous book. "My first time." The beginning of a titillating and most probably embarrassing story told over cocktails to someone the teller doesn't know well enough to tell *anything* to. "My first time." The point of too many movies starring too many hard-bodied nobodies shown on cable television, Friday nights, just past prime time: *The Last American Virgin, Private School, Losin' It, Corky's Hot-Tub Adventure, My Favorite Weekend, Ski Patrol IV: Moguls!, Mommie's Italian Chauffeur, Dad's Swedish Masseuse, Beach Shak Summer, 555-LOVE, Flesh Flood, Initiate This*.

My first time?

Suffice it to say there was one. Although I can't for the life of me remember it.

*   *   *

Rosemary's brother showed up unexpectedly.

He answered Rosemary's door one day when I went over for dinner. "Can I help you?" he asked from behind the chain.

Confused, I faltered. "Rosemary? Uh, is she here?"

"Yes, I'm here," I heard her say. "Good God, Duncan." The man was pulled back, the door unchained and reopened. Rosemary beamed at me. "Hello."

"Hey," I said, uncertain if I should stay or leave.

"Well, come in," she boomed, happily. "I want you to meet my brother."

Duncan, it turned out, was the family's black sheep. He appeared unexpectedly from time to time, bursting with stories of his life as an itinerant blackjack dealer. He'd left home immediately after Lee High graduation to attend gaming school in Las Vegas and since then had been employed by casinos and backdoor card clubs across the nation. Over a six-pack of Shiner he told me he himself had never gambled. "Not once," he insisted. "Not on anything."

"You know the odds too well," I ventured.

"Hell no. No such thing as odds. I'm the world's most unlucky man. Why stir up misfortune?"

At the time, Duncan was traveling from Atlantic City to an Indian reservation somewhere "out West."

"Thought I'd pop in for a stay. Catch up on old times and all that. Say, what happened to your hand?"

"Accident," I said.

"No duh. You're not by any chance the feller that got his hand chomped by a Doberman while robbing an old lady's house, are you?"

"What feller would that be?"

"You know. That feller. You've heard the story, surely."

Rosemary came in with a bowl of queso and a bag of corn chips. "Oh, boy," she groaned. "Here come the stories. Duncan gets the best dumb gossip from around the globe," she explained.

"People have to do something while they piss away their dough," Duncan argued. "How do you think I learned my sister was the Kentucky Fried Rat Lady? I've heard about her in every gambling town I've worked. You're Colonel Sanders's worst nightmare, the bane of every working mother north of the equator." He leaned over to pinch Rosemary's cheek.

"That's not me." Rosemary sighed. "You know the truth."

Duncan took a long sip of beer. "Truth is, the truth's a deadly bore. Always a disappointment. You can bet on it."

Brautigan's wife has driven the kids over to Corpus Christi for their spring break. They're staying in a neighbor's condo.

"It could have been worse," Brautigan whines. "I could have gone out and had an affair."

"That wouldn't have gotten you arrested," I say.

"No charges were pressed," Brautigan mitigates. "And everyone believed I was just doing research."

"Not me. I *know* what you were doing."

There is a long pause. Brautigan doodles on his pad. Finally he says, "I'm afraid I'll do it again."

"This town isn't big enough for the both of us," I drawl.

*   *   *

My freshman year, my homeroom was homeless. That is, we didn't have a regular classroom to call our own. Instead, our teacher, Mrs. Holloway, held court in the massive theater that took up more than an eighth of our WPA-built school but hadn't been used in a number of years due to rotted planks on the stage. (Rumor had it the auditorium was condemned by a former principal immediately after he was fitted for casts on both legs, broken after plunging through the stage floor while delivering a dramatic reading from *A Christmas Carol* the day before Winter Break. He—allegedly—had just finished a sniveling redneck rendition of Scrooge's poorhouse rant when, *crash*, down he went. Students and teachers, ill-read, uncaring, mistook the accident as part of the performance, departed amidst a smattering of applause. When the janitor found him late that afternoon, the principal, confusing his salvation with the Ghost of Christmas Future, begged for another chance.) Each morning Mrs. Holloway, wary of the stage, stood at the front of the auditorium and begged us to remain seated and quiet for the duration of our stay with her. Then she walked to the back of the auditorium and read detective novels while my peers ran wild in the aisles. It was not difficult to get up on the stage, despite a fence of hastily erected barbed wire, and if careful, one could trod the area without fear of broken limbs or impalement. I would venture to say that, of the twelve girls in my homeroom, five of them lost their virginity to Buzz Henry in the upstairs dressing room of that auditorium. While the rest of us studied and copied homework due in the

next class, Buzz was led—very willingly—into that lofty nest to per-
form the act he'd allegedly perfected in sixth grade with a nympho-
maniacal cheerleader from the nearby Junior College. The girls were
not competitive or catty in their use of Buzz. Strangely, they seemed
to have worked out some kind of schedule by which they abided. We'd
hear them sometimes, their faint moans haunting the dank and shadowy room like a forgotten phantom (or feverish principal), ecstasy
muffled by the molding velvet curtains and cooing pigeons nesting
high in the rafters. When the vocal demonstrations were especially
operatic, I would turn to see if Mrs. Holloway had noticed, if she'd
vacated her world of dames and private dicks long enough to sniff out
the drama being performed above and in front of the entire homeroom. But, despite the giggles and whispers and occasional "Attaboy,
Buzz" from a fellow footballer, Mrs. Holloway remained oblivious. On
mornings when Buzz was allowed a period to rest, according to the
schedule's odd calendar of celibate holidays, the rest of us prowled
the stage like cat burglars. Alone usually, we'd run into one another
in the dark, start, then continue creeping from one shadowy corner to
the next. I firmly believe we all wanted to play hide-and-seek but were
afraid to suggest the game, for fear of being branded a child, though
that is precisely what we were.

The day I climbed the stairs to the upper dressing room, curious
to see what the mysterious seraglio contained (a mattress, a couch, a
pillow-filled gondola, what?), it was raining. It drummed the roof
above me, growing louder as I climbed higher and higher into the
cobwebs and shadows. The wooden stairs creaked and trembled be-

neath my tentative steps until at last I stood in front of a wooden door whose knob had been pulled out. Resisting the urge to bend down and look through the hole before entering, I pushed the door wide and, like the hero of some preposterous melodrama, strode through the doorway, chest stuffed full of air, head held high, ready for anything.

But.

There was nothing much. A window through which filtered bluish light. A dozen or so stove-sized wooden boxes. Several balding mops and brooms. Some crudely drawn set pieces: a sitting room, window looking out on a snowy hill; an Old West saloon; a jungle clearing, monkey eternally swinging down from a banana tree; Grecian columns; a ship's wheel manned by a fading chalk navigator, sopping from the storm against which he leaned. In the center of the room, a chaise lounge, wine-colored, springs blooming from its seat like rusting daffodils—Buzz's altar, no doubt—balanced on three legs. Condoms littered the floor, as did de-labeled pint bottles of Jack Daniel's, long empty. A bird's skeleton rested on a bed of its own feathers. This was no seraglio, no Turkish harem strewn with scarves and elephantine silk pillows. This was grim. This was dilapidation itself.

I turned to go, but the boxes caught my eye. There was writing on them that seemed to speak to me, almost summon me. Careful to avoid the shriveled rubbers, I crossed the room to investigate. "A NOBLE EXPERIMENT," one box read. I opened its top and rustled through a pile of time-yellowed lab coats and a convict's striped shirt. The box next to it, labeled "LAST NIGHT ON KRAKATOA," contained a number of grass skirts, innumerable coconut shells, a wildly feathered headdress and an eyeless stuffed parrot. "CHERRY TREE? WHAT

CHERRY TREE?" held four pairs of seven-league boots, a pink dress the size of a circus tent, thirty-six powdered wigs, and a little hatchet, its rubbery blade painted a bright gold. "FANGS FOR THE MEMORIES" was furnished with a thin black cape, a brass candelabrum, an enormous rubber rat (its snout beginning to crumble), and fourteen bloodstained white nightgowns. The writing on the last box was different from the simple block lettering on the others. In elaborate calligraphy, someone had written "JOLLY ROGER FOLLIES."

Among other things, of course, the box contained it.

It.

It, a crescent moon.

It, a midget's scimitar.

It, a silver-plated croissant, ill-conceived boomerang, serious question mark.

It, tarnished, but not rusty beyond hope.

It, mounted on a leather sleeve, looking comfortable even at first sight, even there, in that dingy love shack, even in pigeon-shit-tinged light and air, even so looking like a part of me, missing and restored by luck, by Jove, by fate.

It was love at first sight.

Duncan had a briefcase full of scratch-off lottery tickets from across the country. Since he didn't gamble, they were all untouched. "I give them out to people I meet around. You know, in restaurants, at laundromats. Here," he said, handing me one. "Try it." I looked at the ticket. It featured a square of silver latex imprinted MATCH THREE next to a cartoonish pirate straddling a treasure chest leaking strands of pearls. The chest rested on a bed of doubloons whose sparkling was represented by three lines radiating from the edges of certain coins, like the sun's corona stylized by a seven-year-old. The pirate, of course, had a green-orange-yellow parrot on one shoulder, a patch over his right eye, and (surprise) a hook on his left hand. Behind the pirate, a tiny ship, its cannons, crow's nest and death's-head flag just barely distinguishable, floated amongst flea-sized whitecaps. BUC-CANEER BILLIONS, the top of the ticket read in scarlet Barnum letters. "You may already be a winner," Duncan teased.

I scratched at the dull silver area with the tip of my hook until it was revealed that I had won nothing.

"Too bad," Duncan said. "You had two twenty-five thousands, though. What it was, was: it almost was." He sighed. "That's the way it always is."

Brautigan's office is darkened, shades pulled to reduce the glare off the framed diplomas, citations and pictures of Brautigan—sunburnt, mosquito-bothered—posing next to Aztec pyramids.

"I don't know if I would have done anything," Brautigan says. "I think I just wanted to sit out there, watching it get dark, imagining what it would be like to jump out and scare somebody. But would I have actually done it? If somebody had pulled up, radio blaring Ravel, Tchaikovsky—"

"The Eagles," I add.

"If somebody'd done that, would I have lurched from out of the shadows brandishing my hook?" Brautigan takes off his glasses and polishes them with a handkerchief he pulls out of his rear pocket.

"Well, the hook you have *is* plastic." I'm trying to find a way to counsel the doctor without sounding know-it-allish, do-gooderian, hypocritical. "So it wouldn't have flashed in the moonlight. And I think that's something you need to consider."

"I could get a metal hook," the doctor whispers to himself.

"And, of course, you need to keep in mind that a lot of people carry guns nowadays. Even teenagers. Even the girl teenagers. You never know when you might find yourself—unarmed—at the mercy of a nineteen-year-old with an Uzi."

Brautigan shivers. "I hadn't thought of that."

"It is *le hobby dangereuse*," I conclude.

My *Backpacker* arrives, thick with a "First Time Tent Buyers' Complete Guide" and the scent of a new cologne, Trekker. Musky. Fertile. According to the ad, which is unusually copy-heavy, short on men with smooth, sculpted chests, Trekker is the only cologne approved for camping use by the National Park Service. Bears, it seems, possess incredible olfactory senses. Attracted to anything not smelling like pine trees or dirt, they are keen to attack women wearing perfume, men sporting Old Spice, menstruating co-eds, deodorantized bird-watchers, love-making newlyweds. "Trekker," the ad states, "*is* Nature." Men wearing the stuff come across to your average ursine snout as nothing more than a stack of rocks and birdshit. But women—ah, *les femmes*—perceive Trekker as the odor of the gods. "Trekker. Because sometimes a good campfire just isn't good enough."

It occurs to me, as I peel back the scented strip to whiff Trekker, that these magazine ads, scintillating as they are, would drive a bear insane. Pity the unlucky newsstand owner who sets up shop too close to a wildlife preserve. I picture a grizzly barging up Main Street, drawn to the new Zsa Zsa Gabor fragrance emanating from the March *Panache*, a black bear wreaking havoc at the drugstore, driven mad by Cher's Tatu! in the April *Outlaw*, a polar bear mauling a mail plane carrying five dozen October *Floridian*s and their cargo of Conch: by Mennen. A parade of koalas descends on Madison Avenue, demanding more pungent solicitations. Zoo bears clamor and reach between bars not for a passing tourist's cotton candy but the copy of *Très Très* stuffed in her Dooney & Bourke. Circus bears howl in the night as their freight cars pass sticky-sweet post offices and the waiting cache of Cache.

Before I get down to my perusal of *Backpacker*'s monthly Trail RunDown, I tear the Trekker ad out and take it to my own bear-calling closet. The stack of strips has grown out of its box and rises like a pillar toward the empty coat rod. Trekker's scent mingles with the aroma of its brother ads, is engulfed, disappears when I shut the door.

And then, as I turn, I think I hear someone call my name. That is I *think* I hear someone. The voice, if that's what it is, is inside my head and familiar. Neither female nor male, tenor, bass, soprano, alto, it takes me by surprise. I pause to see if it will continue, but it does not, and I am left wondering if it was ever there at all, if it was just the creak of the closet's door, the squeak of my turning soles. "Hello," I say aloud. Then—inside my head—hello . . .

But I am, so far as I can tell, alone.

*   *   *

While Duncan went to the store to get an eggplant for ratatouille, Rosemary and I lounged on the front porch, listening to the last cars pulling into the drive-in for the night's double feature. It grew quiet, except for a few slamming doors, an occasional bleating horn. The edges of the screen began to glow with coming attractions and snack-bar flirtations. A grasshopper pounced onto the middle of the porch, sat for a moment, then hopped off into the Bermuda and invisibility.

"Orchelimum," I said.

"What's that?"

"Orchelimum. The scientific name for the meadow grasshopper."

"Pretty word."

"Means, 'I dance in the woods.' "

"Mm," Rosemary hummed. "I like that."

We sat in silence for close to a minute. Over at the drive-in, a boy's voice—lost—hollered, "Audrey!"

"Duncan thinks I should go with him." She said it in one breath, expelling it like it was something held inside too long, a pearl-diver's gasp.

My heart shuddered. "What? Where to? What do you mean?"

"West. To the casino at the reservation. He thinks I could maybe get a job teaching there. On the reservation. And he says I would like it a lot. He says it looks like an old John Ford western. The landscape, he means. It would be real different. Mountains and rivers and Indians."

"Well," I said, but I didn't know what to say after that, so I just kept quiet.

"What do you think?" Rosemary said, trying to pull it out of me with a whisper.

"Duncan's crazy." I coughed, half laughing. "You two would kill each other."

"He's my brother."

"Siblings have been known to murder one another. Biblical precedents, once set, breed crimes like those plague locusts lay eggs."

That brought about another long stretch of silence, broken only by the lost boy's now-cracking voice, a mixture of anger and fear. "Audrey," he called, snipping the name short, embarrassed to be howling it like a rancher calling the cows home to dinner.

"Do you want me to go?" Rosemary said. "Or do you want me to stay?"

"Audrey!"

"I think she's gone," I said, raising my voice a bit, not really expecting or wanting the stranded boy to hear me, but needing to say something, wishing somebody would tell him to give it up, break the bad news to him, give him a beer, a joint, a ride home.

Rosemary: "Do you want me to go? Or stay?"

"I want you to do whatever you want to do," I tried, knowing that wouldn't suffice.

"Dubois, Wyoming," Brautigan says.

"Been there. Had a beer at the Rustic Pine Tavern."

"Activity?"

"None. Lonely place that."

"Deadwood, South Dakota."

"Lovely place. Gambling's legal there now, I'm told."

"Activity."

"Yes."

"Lexington, Kentucky."

"Done it."

"Activity."

"Done it."

"Coral Gables, Florida."

"Prettiest beaches I've ever seen. Activity, yes."

"Cupertino, California."

"Never got around there."

"Luling, Texas."

"Home to the Watermelon Thump. Last weekend of every June. Nicest people in the world. Couldn't bring myself to do it."

"Nashville?"

"Missed that one."

"Memphis."

"Yes. Yes."

Brautigan pauses. He's been working like an automaton lately, unwilling to give up the project but deeply afraid of becoming too involved. He crosses his legs, and I notice he's sporting mismatched socks. "Maybe we could take a little break," I suggest.

"Yes," Brautigan agrees. "A breather." He gets up to fetch us Dr Peppers from the machine down the hall. When he comes back in he says—as if completing a thought he'd started before leaving the room—"I never went parking as a kid. Maybe that's it."

"Maybe."

He grimaces. "I can't stop thinking about it. How do you stop thinking about it?"

"Read a good magazine," I suggest. "That helps for a while. Gets your mind off things."

"It's like an addiction." He sits down and leans toward me, lowers his voice. "Last night"—he looks around as if someone may have snuck in without our noticing and sits crouched on the shelves behind his chair—"last night I ordered a pizza, then went outside and sat behind our gardenia bushes, watching cars go by. When the delivery boy came, pimpled gangly lummox, I rustled the leaves a bit, then hopped out like an insane gardener. Boy jumped like a jackrabbit. I told him I'd been looking for my wallet, then pulled it out of my back pocket to pay for the pizza. 'Oh, look,' I told him. 'Found it.' "

"Man alive," I say. "You've got it bad."

"Yes," Brautigan hisses. "And listen to this . . ."

But I can't. I can't focus. While he talks about sneaking up on his own car parked in his driveway—"practice"—I begin to think about my mail. How it's probably just now being slid into my box. A couple of magazines, ripe with perfume strips. A sewage/garbage bill. An Ed McMahon come-on. And a letter from Rosemary. Definitely. Today will be the day. I convince myself it will come today, carrying Rosemary's past with it, into my lonely presence.

*   *   *

What I did mainly in junior high was fade. Fearing that my new disability would make me visible to the point of distraction, I undertook a plan to make myself as unremarkable as possible. I was forced to eliminate sports from my daily agenda. I also cut out talking in class, hanging out in the locker areas before or after school, wearing anything that wasn't bland. Indeed, by the time I was a senior in high school, I had become a sort of invisible man, neither popular or unpopular, almost imperceptible. I made straight B's to avoid the closer scrutiny of teachers worried or excited about my grades, shunned dances, attended athletic events incognito, standing at the rear of crowds or beneath bleachers. The only luxury I allowed myself was a leather jacket, which I kept slung over the offending limb in even the most stifling weather. At the time, those leather jackets were all the rage, allowing me a convenient and believable rationalization. If any of my old classmates still happen to own their yearbooks, and if they should ever have occasion to peruse those glossy pages, they must wonder at my picture. Unable to see the hook in my grim mug shot, they may have no grasp on who I was, who I am. My face, unlike Quasimodo's in that dreadful joke, does not ring a bell.

I recall—now with humor—the boy and girl, class president and vice-president, who approached me one day outside senior English, yawn-making *Ivanhoe* clutched in my good hand. "Hi," they said simultaneously.

"Hello."

"I'm Tricia," the girl said. She spoke a little louder than was necessary, and very slowly, as if talking to a deaf person or an immigrant new to the language. "And this," she pointed to her partner, "is Jimmy."

"Hi," Jimmy said again.

"We're seniors, too," Tricia sang, as if identifying herself to me as a fellow Jehovah's Witness or poodle owner.

"Yes," I said, trying to avoid eye contact with either of them. "I know."

"And," Jimmy boomed, taking over, "we're in charge of making The Banner for graduation." The Banner was an enormous stretch of canvas that hung outside the gymnasium where the graduation ceremonies were held. On it, each senior's nickname was lovingly graffitied under a scarlet "CONGRATULATIONS!" just above a piss-yellow "CLASS OF (whatever) RULES!"

"And the thing is," Jimmy continued, "we just suddenly realized—"

"Time has flown!" Tricia suddenly exploded.

"And we just realized that you don't really have a nickname. And we thought maybe you had some idea . . ."

"Maybe you have a nickname for yourself!" Tricia chirped.

"I don't have a nickname?" I said, amazed.

"How about Lefty?" Tricia suggested. She repeated the name several times to herself while tossing her hair from side to side.

"That's good," Jimmy said.

"*I* don't have a nickname?" I repeated.

"Nope," Jimmy and Tricia choired.

"But I always just assumed . . ."

"Do you have something you'd like to be called? Like a name you always wished your parents had named you instead of what they did? Like I always wanted to be named Pete or Andy."

"Really?" Tricia drawled. "That is so weird, because I always wanted to be called Andrea!"

"I guess . . ."

"Yes," Tricia breathed. I could smell her cinnamony breath.

"I guess you should just put 'The Hook.' "

Jimmy and Tricia remained perfectly still for a moment, each searching the other's face to be sure it was neither of them who had said it.

"Yeah," I concluded, " 'The Hook' will be fine."

"She's taken the kids to San Angelo to shop for school clothes," Brautigan says. We're in his car headed to his house for dinner. This is the first time I've thought about his home, even though it's only a few blocks away from my own. He, in fact, owns my home. It's a rent house he invested in several years after he took his job at the University. For the duration of my stay, he's given me a substantial reduction on rent. "They're staying with her sister tonight. And then shopping like mad tomorrow."

We pull into the driveway of a two-story Victorian monster. "Here we are," Brautigan says while we wait for the door of the garage secreted behind the house to finish its automatic rise. "I guess I should warn you about my wife's wigs," Brautigan begins while he guides the car into the garage. Before he can explain further, I gasp. We're surrounded. The walls of the garage are furnished from floor to ceiling with metal utility shelves. And each shelf, every level, is occupied by featureless white Styrofoam heads, and each Styrofoam head is crowned with a wig. In every color, every texture, every imaginable coiffure, wigs.

"Your wife, she likes wigs?"

Brautigan gets out of the car and reaches through a wall of blond hair flowing off one wig head down in front of the wig head below it. When he pulls his hand out again, he's holding a key. "Well, yes," he says. "These aren't all her wigs, though. She originally intended to set up a mail-order wig business. And these are sample wigs. Some of them she made herself. She took a correspondence course in wig-making. A lot of these are made from horses' manes and tails," he points out.

I look around to see if I can identify the equestrian models. I cannot, although one dreadlocked nest of fiber calls to mind Black Beauty in one of his less flattering moments.

"It, uh, never really got off the ground. Her business. But she couldn't bear to get rid of the wigs, and nobody seemed interested in buying them as a lot. I thought she might offer them to some wig museum. The interesting ones, that is. She grew one of them in the backyard. Cornsilk, or hemp, or something like that."

"It's a very striking tableau," I say.

Brautigan nods, then lowers his voice. "Scary as hell at night."

Using the key he fished from behind the hairy waterfall, Brautigan lets us in the back door. "It's sort of a mess," he apologizes. "But it always is. It's not just that the wife and kids have left me here to bach it." He switches on a light and reveals a realm of pinecones. Everywhere. Hundreds of them. In piles on a card table. Scattered across kitchen counters. Hanging from threads taped to the ceiling fan. Following Brautigan as he makes his rounds—checking phone messages (none); fetching the mail (a dry cleaner's coupon)—I discover pinecones in every imaginable nook and cranny. The house is awash in them.

"Pinecones."

"What?" Brautigan is poking around under the sink for charcoal lighter and matches. "What? Pinecones? Oh, yes. They're like Tribbles. You ever see that *Star Trek*? Good one. Kyle collects them. Pinecones, that is." He stands up with a squeeze-bottle of Flame-Now and a box of matches. "Each one is tagged. Place collected. Date. He's been picking them up for years and has pen pals all over the world who supply him with the truly exotic varieties."

I look around trying to see if I can distinguish the exotic varieties from the domestic. They all look so familiar, so pineconish, I am at a loss. Noticing one preserved under a glass globe, I say, "Wow. There's a nice one," and nod at it.

"That's the first one," Brautigan explains. "He picked it up in the front yard when he was a baby and carried it around for four years solid. They were inseparable. Some babies bond with their blankets, some with pinecones. If you look closely, you can see where one of his baby teeth broke loose and is wedged between two whatsits." Brautigan leans toward me a little, grinning. "He named it Ollie."

*   *   *

During the course of the evening I manage to excuse myself several times from our vigil at the barbecue pit. Under the guise of pea-sized-bladder discomfort, I set off for "the bathroom" again and again. Behind various doors I discover a number of incredible collections. In a bedroom painted shocking pink I find bookshelves o'erflowing with soup cans, all unopened.

In the cavernous attic rumpus room, floor a logjam of Tinkertoys and LEGOS, the walls are covered in Polaroid pictures, hundreds and hundreds of them, closeups of people's faces, each individual sporting reading glasses and a broad smile. One room is stacked high with canoe paddles; another swims in ceramic fishes.

It is only during my last expedition that I discover the good doctor's study, wherein grows a forest of his legal pads and spiral notebooks, stacked one atop another from the scratched hardwood floor to the creamy stucco ceiling. Taking one pad from the nearest stack, pulling it out gingerly, giving no thought to how I might reinsert it, I open it to find a transcription of a conversation we'd had early in our work together, when Brautigan was obsessed with finding out if the position of the stars had anything to do with my actions, if the moon affected my stalkings as it affected the tides and werewolves.

Brautigan: What can you tell me about the Big Dipper?

Subject: No matter where I look, I find it.

Brautigan: So, it's your *special* constellation.

Subject: No, I just don't know any others. Hell, I don't know if I'm seeing the Big Dipper right. It's like playing connect-the-dots on a dalmation; if it stands still long enough, you can find anything you want.

Brautigan: Anything?

Subject: Sure.

Brautigan: Could you find a rooster?

Subject: A rooster? Is that supposed to mean something? Is that supposed to say something about my mental state?

Brautigan: No. It's just the first thing that came to mind.

Subject: What made you think rooster?

Brautigan: I don't know. What do you think that means?

Subject: Are you asking me for real, or is this some kind of trick?

Brautigan: For real.

Subject: Roosters don't lay eggs.

Brautigan: And?

Subject: Foghorn Leghorn is a blithering fool.

Brautigan: Meaning?

Subject: (thirty seconds of silence) You know, now that I think about it, once, while skulking—unsuccessfully—near Lawrence, Kansas, I'm almost positive I found Orion.

Notepad tucked in the waistband of my underwear, at the small of my back, I go out to find Brautigan standing in the middle of a roped-off area at the rear of the yard. "We're putting in a storage building back here. Nothing big."

"Oh, really," I say. "With a nice big house like you've got?"

"It gets a tad crowded sometimes. Hence the need for a little extra space."

"Your family has an interesting collection of . . . collections."

I watch Brautigan's face to see if he can tell what I've been up to, what I've witnessed, what I know.

"Yes. We all have our own interests."

"I'll say. You, yourself, what exactly do you collect?"

Brautigan's brow descends to hood his eyes. "I suspect," he says, spitting a little, "the steaks are done." Like a count welcoming guests to his castle, he sweeps wide his arm, ushering me toward the heat-spitting fire. "Shall we dine?"

Rusty's latest postcard to DeeDee appeared today, sandwiched between a phone bill and a True Value Dollar Daze flyer. On it, a girl in a hoop skirt, lavender parasol resting lightly against her milky shoulder, poses in a garden crowded with magnolias and oleanders. In the background, cypress trees curtained in Spanish moss tower spookily. The girl's eyes, a lab-doctored blue, blaze out of the postcard like the pilot light on my stove. Her hair, Andalusian eddies, swirls, waves and dips, glistens like black ice. The gargantuan dress she models is polar bear white, trimmed with snowflake lace, swooping satin w's, veins of glacial ribbons from which tinkle and sparkle pea-sized bells. Her waist, narrow as a champagne flute, rises stiffly from the Monticello-ish hoop. Her bodice swells to showcase an ample bosom, adorned with a galaxy of sea-stolen pearls. Sleeves billow like cumulonimbus. Her smile, a knife blade of hospitality, demonstrates an upbringing lousy with visits to the family orthodontist. Is there a Civil War cannon hidden under the belle's bulky skirt? Does the family rottweiler crouch there in that musky tent, eager to rip the balls off a marauding Yankee?

Are alligators poised, teeth glinting, to attack, signaled by her sweetly drawled "Chee-eeese" and the camera's minuscule click? Does a hurricane lurk just behind the photographer's sunburnt neck, charitably delaying its onslaught for the sake of Beauty's capture?

"DeeDee," writes Rusty, "Be glad you're in West Texas where an occasional breeze comes up. This here is some kind of hell. Ready to come back home to you. Always yours."

We drove to Dallas to shop for a hand. On Main Street just east of downtown, in an area called Deep Ellum due to the locals' pronunciation of nearby Elm Street as Ellum, a simple, neat storefront housed (and may still house) "Lemon's Prosthetics."

"Are you nervous?" my mother asked me as we drove through downtown Big D. My left foot stamped an allegretto tatoo on the muddied floorboard of our faithful Ford.

I didn't lie. Between my mother and me even bravery was no excuse for a maltreatment of truth. "Yes," I said. "But excited, too."

My doctor had given us the address of the place, had phoned ahead and spoken to Mrs. Delia Lemon, proprietor, explained the situation and needs and limited budget on which we survived. "I hope they have something we can afford," I said.

"They do," my mother assured me. "We're not leaving until we've haggled our way into the most extravagant and marvelous fist in existence." She reached over with her free hand (such luxury, two hands) and stilled my thumping foot, knee, leg. "Maybe we'll get one with diamond rings built into it."

"Yuck," I said.

"Or maybe one that, at the push of a button, will constrict to squeeze a cute girl's elbow—"

I blushed and smiled. "Nah."

"Or a beer can. You could flatten beer cans without batting an eye. Think how handy that might be in college."

We both knew I wouldn't be going to college most probably, unless I stumbled upon some deluxe financial aid. But I laughed anyway. "Maybe they'll have a hand that heats up. I could warm rolls and cook eggs in my palm."

"Or a foreign hand, one modeled on the reigning extremity of an African king. Or a Japanese hand, designed to excel at judo. I bet they make a million kinds of hands. Dainty, French manicured hands for debutantes. Slender but masculine hands with long fingers for piano players—"

"Former piano players," I amended.

"*Piano* players," my mother insisted. "Rough, burly lumberjack hands—probably a huge market for those."

And then, suddenly, we were there, pulling up to the curb at a store whose windows were so clean they appeared to be not there at all. The dust-free sidewalk was shadowed by a bright yellow awning that extended away from the building all the way to the street. Lemon's Prosthetics. The words floated on the door's glass. From where I sat, I could see a woman with red hair standing behind a desk, waving at us. Smiling.

"I think I expected something less bright," my mother said.

"Someplace dark and dank, below street level," I added.

The woman inside picked up what looked like a mannequin's hand off her desk and waved it at us.

"Something nearly invisible," I said. "Someplace secret."

Things get out of control quickly.

Like second-graders defending their favorite superheroes or most lovingly despised comic-book villain, the students have worked themselves into a cursing tizzy. The threat of violence exists. I am sitting at the back of the room again, observing the frantically expanding hostilities and Brautigan's seeming enjoyment of the whole shebang.

It started out simply enough. A pair of students gave a short presentation on two modern folkloric characters: myself and the dreaded Axe Man, a killer who dresses up like a little old lady to wait in mall-shoppers' darkened parked cars. The presentations were, in my opinion, entertaining, but—at least the parts about me—a tad sketchy. The conclusion met with patchy applause and foot-stomping.

"Good," Brautigan allowed, "insofar as you related the tales fairly and included relevant regional variations. But you've neglected a fairly obvious means of delving deeper into the meanings behind the men. How do they compare?" Silence. "Anyone?"

"The Hook Man is better," a girl in the front row announced, inducing a smile on her very hero's lips.

"Not," a Hispanic youth sitting directly behind her countered. "The Hook Man is lame. He doesn't do nothing."

"Yeah," the boy sitting next to him added. "Plus, I've heard that story ten million times. I'd never heard about the Axe Man before."

"So, what? Are you guys saying new is better?" a girl with frizzy black hair asked. "Like New Coke was better than Coca-Cola Classic? Get a grip."

"I think the Axe Man is better because he's real clever, you know."

"Like, if the Hook Man put on a dress then he could compete with this flake?"

"What makes transvestitism clever? Hello?"

"Definitely Hook Man," a boy in a backward baseball cap pronounced. People stopped to listen to him, but he just shrugged. "Definitely Hook Man," he repeated.

"Hook Man is perverse, though. He gets after couples doing it, man. At least the Axe Man just gets consumers."

"But the consumers are always women. He's sexist."

"Like he can tell what kind of car a woman drives and that's the one he gets into? Who's being sexist now?"

"The Hook Man wins because he doesn't actually get caught, you know."

"Yeah, but he loses the Hook, man."

"The Axe Man doesn't get caught, either."

"Well, he must have gotten caught once, because we know he's a man, right?"

"Maybe he *got* somebody, and they lived to tell that it was a man."

"As far as I know, the Hook Man never actually got anybody."

"Then why was he in an asylum for the mentally criminal, or whatever?"

(By the way, I have never been in a home of any kind.)

"Axe Man is more urban. That's one thing. The Hook Man hangs out on country roads and shit. He's, like, a nature boy. Axe Man is just a crazy mall-walker, when you get right down to it."

"How come they're both men? Why no Hook Woman or Axe Girl?"

Things went along like that for quite some time. Then they got worse. Name-calling was introduced into the arena. Sides began to be drawn up. The room polarized. One side for me, the other for Axe Man.

Oddly, I'm sitting on Axe Man's side.

And it's very tempting to leap up on top of my desk, brandish my piece and let havoc rule.

But no.

"Ladies and gentlemen," Brautigan half yells. "I would like to introduce one unthought-of theorem into the pudding." The class quieted to mumbles and growls. "What if Hook Man and Axe Man are the same man?"

"No!" I exclaim.

The class is turning toward me as one. Their faces are in profile when (O! joyous cliché!) the bell rings and they return to their normal lives as boys and girls eager to get outside and toss Frisbees, mix margaritas.

Brautigan and I are left alone. He sits at his desk, chair leaning back against the chalkboard. I'm halfway out of my seat. "No," I tell him in a firm voice, the voice I might use to train a dog. "No."

After a solid hour of measuring the circumference of my wrist, elbow, biceps, the length of my forearms, the width of my shoulders, Delia Lemon said, "I've got cotton-mouth. Do you want a Coke?"

I was so caught up in the feel of her skin against my own, her fingernails whispering across my scarred flesh, the smell of her perfume and sound of her kittenish voice reciting the numbers aloud before writing them down, I scarcely heard her. I was hypnotized.

"I would love a Coke," my mother said. I started in my seat, surprised by the sound of her voice, embarrassed to have been thinking the thoughts I was.

"How about you?" Delia Lemon asked, her breath breezing up my nostrils to immobilize my brain. "A Coke?"

I nodded. "Uh-huh."

"Well," Delia said to my mother, "if you don't mind, there's a little grocery just a couple of blocks down. If you tell the man at the counter it's for me, he'll put it on my tab."

"Which way?" my mother said, standing.

"Turn right outside the door. Toward downtown."

"Be right back," my mother promised. And left.

The night of the day my hand came off, I slept in the bottom bunk. This was not the norm. Being the older brother, I had always commanded the privilege of sleeping in the top bunk. In the winter, the heat from our gas stove rose to the ceiling, then settled in layers from the top down; the top bunk was warmer. In the summer, the drafts from the fan that rotated high above the floor were more effectively felt from the top bunk; it was cooler. The top bunk afforded a better, eagle's-eye view of the room. Lounging in the top bunk could lead one to believe he was aslumber in India, in a monkey-filled banyan tree.

Sleeping there was slightly more dangerous than sleeping in the bottom bunk; one might roll out of bed in the course of an enthusiastic dream and dash one's brains against the hardwood floors. The top bunk, by the very nature of its name, was better. It was mine.

My little brother tried to make his bottom bunk into a more desirable locale by transforming it, using sheets and blankets, into a cave accessible only to him. Rather than allow him any sense of victory, I shunned the whole idea of the cave and never attempted to enter when he took refuge therein. It was "stupid," "retarded," and "baby stuff," I recall saying.

Nonetheless, my first handless night, my mother insisted my brother and I trade beds. She was convinced I would be more comfortable in the bottom bunk. Although climbing into the upper bunk was by no means a treacherous feat, my mother worried I would be unable to make the ascent successfully and, once there and sleeping, suddenly, by virtue of my wound, the most likely candidate the world over for tumbling mid-snore from the bunk's daredevil height.

Surprisingly, my little brother did not lord his lucky acquisition over me with nearly the amount of glee I expected. He did, in fact, whine that he would be unable to rest at ease in the top bunk. He was too used to the bottom bunk's womblike embrace. To sleep in the top bunk would be like sleeping outdoors, atop a hill, without tent or sleeping bag. Naked. Vulnerable.

He argued well but unsuccessfully.

When I was comfortably ensconced in my brother's former nest, I smelled him on the sheets and pillows, the sour scent of his nightmare sweat and lemonade breath. "Hey," he said a few minutes after we

were alone, when our parents' voices adjourned to their muffling bedroom.

"What?"

"You know my cow skull?" he said, referring to a recent discovery
he'd made that I silently but obviously coveted. It was stashed in an
old trunk in the barn's tack room where my brother kept the treasures
he considered too valuable for public viewing or too gruesome for my
mother's approval.

"Yeah."

"You can have it if you want it."

I knew what he was doing, of course. And I was honestly touched.
We'd always gotten along, my brother and I. But his offering was the
first time I knew that he felt any affection for me or I for him.

"No," I said. "Thanks, though."

Delia Lemon said, "This is not a very fun way for a thirteen-year-old
boy to spend a nice fall afternoon. Cooped up with me. Getting poked
and prodded and felt up like a piece of meat."

"I'm twelve," I said. "And it's not so bad."

Her hand was warm against the inside of my elbow. I could feel
her pulse thrumming against my own.

"You're doing real well," Delia cooed. "Very brave." Her hand wandered up the inside of my arm to rest on my shoulder. "And you're
very handsome. Did you know that? That you're very handsome?"

I felt like I might pass out. It was not like romance novels would
have you believe, all sounds stopping but for the melody of the be-

loved's voice and the thunderous boom of one's heart. Indeed, sounds
became so loud I thought my head might explode. The air conditioner,
hidden somewhere behind and above me, roared. Fluorescent lights
buzzed like a plague of wasps. Cars passing on the street revved and
whooshed, dragsters and missiles.

"No," I said. I didn't know I was handsome. I don't think for a
moment, actually, that I was. I'm still not.

"But you are," Delia insisted. "You're going to be a very dashing
man. And this"—she didn't need to look down at or point out my
handicap—"doesn't make you any less attractive. For some women,
maybe for all women, it makes you even more exciting. Virile. Adven-
turous."

Delia's hand floated up to caress my cheek. I shut my eyes, afraid
to see what might happen next.

My mother entered the store like a sonic boom. "I'm back," she
announced. I didn't realize I'd been holding my breath, but I had, and
it all rushed out of me at once, as if I was one of those old woodcuts
you see, where the wind, lumpily personified in a cloud, blusters at a
many-masted galleon. "What?" my mother said, her right arm cradling
three sweating sodas. "Are you in pain?"

My mail carrier did not come today.

This is no holiday. It's a Monday.

I put a subscription renewal card for *Texas Monthly* in my mailbox
early this morning, and it's still there. Frustrated, downright angry, I
take the envelope out of the mailbox and walk it down to the post

office. It slides into the empty box with a short whoosh and drumlike thud.

On the way home, I get the strangest feeling that I'm being followed, like in the movie version of *To Kill a Mockingbird*: I think I hear the whisper of footsteps behind me. And when I stop to listen, they stop, too, only a millisecond behind my stopping, so the disparity registers audibly. It becomes a cruel and spooky game, me walking then suddenly stopping, ears poised.

When I'm passing the park, with its tall, thick wall of oleanders bordering the sidewalk, I feel certain the footsteps rush to catch up with me. My heart, in turn, races. Someone's in the oleanders, not more than five feet away from me. I'm sure of it.

I stop. "Hey," I say and wait for a response of some kind, a yelp, a war cry, a raspy breath. "Cecil Jacobs is a big wet hen," Scout called in *Mockingbird*. The same dangerous silence answered her.

One oleander leaf brushes against another. A pink bloom bumps through a maze of branches to the ground. Dirt squeaks under a shifting loafer.

"Who's there?" I ask.

Far off I hear two cars racing down the town's main drag.

"Brautigan?" I ask. "Brautigan? Is that you?"

But there's no more motion. No more night-sounds. My heart slows, and I turn to walk again. Toward home. I don't look back, not once, not even when I'm at my door. I go inside and straight to bed. Without checking closets or nailing a loop of garlic to my headboard, I undress and slide beneath the covers to sleep.

*   *   *

I find Dr. Brautigan in the bathroom, leaning on a washbasin, gazing into a mirror as if remembering a Shakespeare sonnet. "I've been reading," he says when he notices my reflection. "About our ancestors." He waits to see if I will question him. "They were called highwaymen for a time, when people used to travel by carriage or stagecoach. Sometimes . . . they just leapt out at passing vehicles with no intention of robbing them. Sometimes they would *just leap out*. Like the Boogeyman."

"No," I say. "There's no such thing as the Boogeyman. Or if there is, he is something else entirely."

"There are lots of us," Brautigan suggests. "I've been trying to figure out why there are hundreds of reports of you in the Northeast when you claim never to have gone any further north than Ohio. And it's because there is, there has been, there will be *more than one of you*. There's more than one of you in this bathroom."

"There's the me in the mirror and the me in that other mirror and there's just plain me," I say.

"And there's me," Brautigan finishes. "And my reflections, too."

"There's a gang of us," I note. I look at the wall above Brautigan's head, where someone has penciled in large, neat letters, "I THINK, THEREFORE I SPAM."

Brautigan follows my eyes and reads the sentence out loud, then half laughs, half gags. "Where would I be now if I'd decided to concentrate on latrinalia?"

"Same place," I answer. "Everybody ends up here."

*   *   *

There's a note on my mailbox when I get home. The UPS man has been here and in my absence left a package across the street at my neighbor's. I turn and look at where she stands in her yard watering the impatiens that fashion a thick pink-white-green margin around her home. She waves. "Hellooo!" she moos. "I have a box for yoooo."

I wave back and smile. "Can I come get it now?" I ask. Adrenaline begins to pump in my veins. What is it? A gift from Rosemary? A hand-made afghan or tray of divinity? Portrait? Pottery? Elderberry wine?

She beckons to me with her hose, the spray of water fanning out under a rainbow. "It's heavy!" she announces. "Can hardly lift it."

I trot across the street, grinning. "Thanks," I say. "He probably could have just left it on my porch."

"And have some klepto dog-walker make off with it? No." She puts her hose down and dries her hands on the front of her shirt, confiding, "Garden duds."

I hold her front door open for her. "Thank yoooo," she says. Then, "Have you ever seen my house?" I shake my head no. "Well, you'll just have to let me give you the grand tour."

The box is just inside the door, brown cardboard, the size of a small carry-on bag. Before I can bend down to examine it, my neighbor's tugging at my sleeve. "And I just made up a big pitcher of Texas Tea. Do you imbibe?"

"Yes, I do," I say, craning my neck to look back at the diminishing package. The handwriting on the label looks familiar, but I can't make it out. "On occasion."

"My husband was a bartender immediately after we finished college," my neighbor—it occurs to me that I don't even know her name—informs me. "And he taught me the secret to mixing a perfect Texas Tea. Just before he died." She stops. We're in the kitchen, in front of a counter empty but for a tall pitcher of what looks like tea, two glasses, and a wood-grained ice bucket heaped with Texas-shaped cubes. My neighbor points at the pitcher with one hand, shields her mouth with the other, as if keeping a secret from the waiting refreshments. ("Waiting?" Was she waiting for me? Has all this been arranged? Is she aware of my schedule? Am I watched by those around me? Am I paranoid?) "Just a little less tequila than vodka. And a teensy bit less vodka than gin. And a little bit more of everything else, equally. Have you ever been to the R&R Toltec? That's the bar my Rudy tended way back when. And do you know who was the bouncer there at that time?"

"No, ma'am," I say.

She busily begins putting little Lone Star ice cubes into the glasses. "Dan Blocker," she says reverentially.

"Oh, really?"

She hears the confusion in my voice and turns to give me a bewildered look as she pours my tea. "Hoss. Hoss Cartwright. On *Bonanza.*"

"Oh," I say, giving the syllable the proper inflection.

"That's right, 'Oh.' He could toss a drunkard out the door like shooting socks into the laundry hamper."

She hands me my drink and promptly picks up her own to clink it against mine. "Cheers," she chirps. "Now. This is the kitchen, of course."

"Nice," I croon, because it's the right thing to say and it honestly *is* nice, bright and clean and lived-in.

"And through here," my neighbor scurries away, motioning for me to follow, "is the den."

We've already seen the entirety of the downstairs and admired two of the children's old upstairs bedrooms (livestock trophies and twirler's ribbons intact and dustless after more than thirty years) when I begin to realize what is odd about the decor. In every room—every single room, including the laundry and huge walk-in pantry—there are framed, wall-mounted photos of the house itself, sometimes of the very room in which we stand. Going up the staircase a series of photos, some in black and white, others in bright Kodacolor, stagger upward, Stygian. In some rooms, the photos are almost imperceptible, tiny, three by five or smaller, tucked away next to calendars and mummified Homecoming corsages. In other areas, most notably my neighbor's colossal peach-shaded bedroom, the pictures are prominently displayed. Over her well-fluffed pillows, my neighbor has hung a billboard-sized watercolor depicting her and (I assume) her late husband sitting in bed, legs and waists buried under a tangerine comforter, torsos, arms and heads erect, stiff, and elegantly pajamaed in full view of the painter and subsequent witnesses. A cat's haunches and tail sneak in at the bottom left corner. In the master bath a child's finger painting of the shower, portrayed at full blast, a roaring waterfall, midnight blue, is under glass above the toilet. In the study the bookcases are beautifully arranged in both real life and the bizarre

photorealist mural that spans one entire wall. On the landing, an an-
tique stitchery ("Home Sweet Home," of course) is side by side with
an eleven-by-fourteen glossy of that same stitchery. Downstairs again,
in the foyer, glass empty, ready to claim my prize and leave, I look up
to see a last photo above the door, this one of the yard, from the
viewpoint of the porch. Across the street, my house and—in the front
window—a shadowy figure caught against the drapes like the villain
in a magic lantern show, me.

"Thanks for the Tea," I say, the drink's potency thickening my
tongue. "And the tour. You have a beautiful home."

My neighbor lowers her head to beam at her feet. "Do you really
think so?"

"I do. I do," I assure her, like a stuttering groom. Bending, I gather
my package and find myself grunting under its weight.

"It's heavy, I told you," my neighbor reminds me. "Can you get it?
Should I get a dolly?"

"No," I say, face reddening with strain and anticipation for when
the package is in my home and I can have my way with its taped lid.
"I got it."

My neighbor holds the door open for me. "Come back anytime you
get thirsty," she gurgles as I stumble past her, out onto her soaking
lawn. My shoes sink in Bermuda, and I fear losing a shoe. "I'll make
us some more Tea. Or a Scorpion. Do you like Scorpions?" she calls
to me as I cross the street.

I'm at my front door, fumbling with the knob, which I was wise
enough to unlock before my across-the-street adventure. "I love
them," I holler back. And then I'm inside. And the package is before

me on the floor. And I'm pushing the sharp tip of my hook under its taped-shut skin, ready to rip and behold and revel . . .

. . . When I notice for the first time the addressee is *not* yours truly. DEEDEE EASTEP is scrawled across the mailing label in a hand I thought was familiar because indeed it was. Rusty. It's a package from Rusty to DeeDee.

I pause. Should I continue? It's a federal offense to open somebody else's mail. The postcards I haven't had to open. They were postcards. The writing was open-air, alfresco, naked for all the world, all the mail carriers, all the snooping neighbors and lurking landlords to see and read and, if the mood hit them, memorize, as I have memorized all of Rusty's maudlin doodles. But this, this box before me, its lip in my pointy clutch, is another matter entirely. It is a cocoon, secreting a message, one meant to blossom and fly in the face of its intended only.

"Fuck it," I say out loud. I tear the box top up without a second thought, without a pang of guilt. I delve my hand and hook deep into the box's tissue-paper entrails and dredge for treasure. When my hand brushes something at once soft and hard and my hook knocks against an object definitely hard I am confused. But rather than indulge myself in any silly guessing games, I clutch and lift and pull into daylight first a large black rock, then a thick slice of tree trunk. Then my hand goes back into the box, feeling for a third treasure or a note of explanation, long-winded epistle of love.

But there's nothing else.

I sit back to contemplate my plunder.

*   *   *

"I've heard them all," Duncan revealed to me one evening pre–late show. Rosemary snoozed on the sofa. "Standing behind a half-moon of evergreen felt, shuffling decks, throwing aces, scooping chips, awarding silver dollars, changing green bills to yellow, purple, black, red, orange wafers, sporting bow ties, tuxedo shirts, ruffled cuffs, lacy garters, lime eyeshades, winking at bejeweled wives and know-nothing newlyweds, dreamy brides, show-off grooms, eating all-you-can buck ninety-nine buffets, sucking smoke and bad cologne and coffee breath and spilled Amaretto sours, ankles bitching, hands cramping, stomach rumbling, ears ringing from jackpot cacophonies, squealing call girls, cursing grandmaws, bellowing drunks, hissing pit bosses, eyes flooded from retina-stinging neon, running lights, spangles, sparkles, rhinestones, lamé, cubic zirconia, nine-carat diamonds, rubies, opals, have I mentioned lamé, worldview lashed to shreds by marble juggling roulette, hypnotic slots, boisterous craps crowds, cover bands, microphones, mirrors (one-way two-way marbleized), video cameras catching nothing but my hands and the hands of the marks I serve. Over all that I've heard them all. In the midst of the orgy, the circus, the chaos, I have listened and heard, like I said, them all." Duncan paused to breathe. "That's not where they start, but that's where they spread, see, the terror tales and goofball epics: poodles in microwaves, roaches in pop bottles, maniacs on the upstairs extension, spiders in bouffants, cobras in cloth coats. Listen: girl goes to a store, buys a new dress, classy black for the senior prom, feels dizzy during din-din, drops like a rock during an erection-crushing slow dance. Is she pregnant? Brain-tumored? Overcome by teen angst? No. Listen: turns out the dress was worn by a corpse, then exchanged at the last minute by a lunatic undertaker. Formaldehyde soaked into the dress from the corpse, into the girl from the dress. Boom. The mystery is solved. But more importantly, the gross-out is complete. Heard that one from the girl's brother's college roommate's mother-in-law, I shit you not. Harrah's, Lake Tahoe. People gamble. Talk. Try to one-up each other. Later they get on a plane to go home and tell their barber the story they heard. He tells it to another schmo later that afternoon getting his locks lopped for a business trip to St. Louis. *He* tells it to the guy sitting next to him on the plane, who tells it to his kids, who tell it to their dealer, etc. These stories, they're like a harmless but unstoppable virus. Everybody is susceptible, even the skeptical. Sometimes I'll hear some cockamamie gang initiation baloney between hands, and the next week it gets printed in the newspaper as truth. Except the gang's name is changed. Maybe it's a different body part they have to chop off. Casinos are the breeding ground for more than greed, amigo. And you, with your silvery death grip, are old potatoes, greasy kids' stuff, not so hot these sun-crazed post-atomic days, I'm telling you. Tired but not retired, you're a well-loved golden oldie, daddy-o, a cobwebby Tomorrowland attraction people refuse to let go of, but pass up in a minute if the line's short at Space Mountain. But hey, no offense meant. Like they say, keep on trucking."

Rusty's rock is riddled with scratches reminiscent of cave paintings, primitive stick-figure men, women and four-legged beasts. The men thrust spears at the beasts, the women thrust their pointy breasts at the men, the beasts—what are they? buffalo? horses? one appears to be a giraffe, another an orangutan—run at the women, away from the spears, toward a crude crescent moon curving around the rock's top, bottom, side; there is no way to tell which way is up with this thing. I roll it end over end on the floor, looking for some pattern, some way to read the chase that will explain why Rusty would want DeeDee to have this.

Giving up for the moment, I turn to the chunk of wood, bark whittled away. Every inch of it is covered in words burned into it with—presumably—an electric pen. Holding it like a scroll that refuses to unroll, I attempt to read it, but can't. The words—if they are words—are scrambled, letters apparently rearranged, sometimes smushed together in front of a reddish knot, some huge capitals, some tiny lowercase.

EstaNochEfuerademiventanalosOSosCazanelnectardepicaflores
LaLUZDELASEStrellasempolvalaseSpaldastrompasorejasdelica
dasAPreTOlaMANosobrEELpechoaTRAPadoelcorazonqueseHAF
ORzadoporlasCOSTillaspideelpezondeLIBRARlolososohusmean
enlasVENTanasMORDISCANELPINOQUEHACEcentINelaenmi
puertaelcorazonme DICE queteoyellamarminombreME DICEqu
etepuerdeencontrartellevaraaquiparaverlossenalesdelosososenel
pinoparaquelaluzdelasestrellasempolvelasespaldasparaoirlasA
LASdepicaFLOresestaesmicorA ZONE

  elrioquehoINVENTadoyquecorreycorreporlasmontanacontA
NDOnuestrahiSTORiaclamecOrAzonesilencioDUEremelounico
queoyescorazonsonlosososcazandoNEcTARBAjolasEstreELLasco
mEtonOIsywat ERandrePLacEthesunSCOldarMSwiTHYOuroWN

What the hell?

It was, before it was a lake, an oil field dappled with licorice-black derricks, elongated steelwork pyramids named Bub's Gusher #3, Old Faithful South, Woody's Crude Heaven 77. Rosemary and I paddled from one derrick to another, gliding like the water moccasins all around us under the struts and joints and rusting machinery. "I love this place," Rosemary said again and again, turning to smile at me. I sat in the rear, steering, my hook locked onto the paddle like a vise. It was new to me, this paddling and steering and splashing. I hadn't had much to do with water since my accident and my father's death. For fear of rusting my prosthesis, and without the old man's insistence on sitting like mannequins on a muddy bank, cane poles in hand, hands stinking of bloodbait, I had abandoned swimming and fishing and wading and tadpole harassing. On my forays into the American wilds, I had seen much water: rivers, lakes, ponds, puddles of every dimension and color. Indeed, one late July eve I surprised two employees of a waterpark—Wet Dreams, USA—only moments before they would have shimmied out of their skimpy red uniforms. (My hook, framed in the triangle of a rear passenger window, my adrenaline pumping like mad, the shriek echoing over and over across the asphalt parking lot, the smell of chlorine permeating it all, giving way to the pungent aroma of rubber burning: a successful venture, in every regard.)

"Over there," Rosemary said, pointing her paddle at a derrick that loomed just right of us, twenty yards away. I struggled to maneuver the canoe around. My shoulders ached, my back ached, my chest ached, but I was happy nonetheless to bring even more pain onto myself; Rosemary's smile wooed me like a snake charmer's penny whistle. I was careful not to splash too much, careful to keep the paddle at the side of the canoe, to bring it up and out of the water slowly and put it back in gently, to keep the water quiet, to maintain the "peace" Rosemary praised so highly every five minutes or so. A trout or bass, some mysterious lake-dweller, somersaulted after a mosquito behind us, his splash so much different than my own, his splash belonging here, a part of this wild puzzle, my own being unwanted, an intruder's. "What was that?" Rosemary said, turning around.

"Bass," I answered, pretending great knowledge of things masculine and scaly. "Largemouth."

"Slow down," Rosemary bid me, turning back to her position as scout.

I held my paddle still in the water, dragging us slower and slower as we approached one derrick. "I think this is the tallest, don't you?" Rosemary asked. Without waiting for an answer, she threw the rope around the rig's algaed leg and began to clamber up onto the ladder of crossing iron bars. Though footless, she was as surefooted as a bighorn sheep. Halfway to the top, she stopped and looked down at me. "Come on."

Wary of the boat's shifting center of balance, I made my way to the same spot from which Rosemary had begun her ascent. I dislodged the paddle from my hook's grip. My shoulder ached with relief, unaware of the coming new challenge. "Careful," I called up to Rosemary, a warning meant as much for myself.

"You, too," she sang back.

My hook clanged against the metal like a drumstick against a fine Turkish cymbal. Each gonging signaled another step up, like the tintinnabulations of an elevator moving from Bargain Basement to Sporting Goods to Lingerie.

Clang. Clang. Clang.

By now, Rosemary had reached the top of the derrick. She'd swung herself astraddle one wide beam, cowgirlishly, her shorts a nightmare of rust stains. "What can you see?" I asked her, half hoping she would declare the view unsatisfactory and begin her descent.

"Everything," she said. "Come up here."

Clang. Clang. Clang.

I stopped again, several feet short of where Rosemary perched. "Can you see water moccasins? I bet you can see lots of water moccasins."

Without looking down, Rosemary grinned. I couldn't see it, but I could hear it in her voice. "Come on up," she said, the space between each word like a finger curling, beckoning.

Clang. Clang. Clang.

"I think maybe I've climbed high enough. I think I can probably see everything just as clearly from right here," I said, even though I'd looked at nothing but the canoe below me and the iron rails I clutched.

"Get up here," Rosemary said, perturbed.

Clang. Clang. Clang.

And then, at last, I *was* there, face to face with Rosemary. I swung my leg across the same beam on which she sat and balanced myself carefully.

"You're not looking at where I'm looking," Rosemary complained.

"I'm looking at you."

Rosemary grabbed my shoulders and twisted me around. "Turn," she said, meaning it. I cautiously raised myself up so that I could rotate to look at whatever it was Rosemary found so important for me to see. It was the setting sun, of course, as red and yellow and orange and gold as any painter or poet ever described it.

"Look at the water," Rosemary said. She put her hands on my shoulders again and pulled me toward her, so that I had to scoot backward to keep from being pulled down. When I felt my back meet her bosom, I stopped. She took her hands from my shoulders and clasped them around my belly, like a pulsing, luxurious belt. "Look at the water," she said again. "See."

"I don't feel very well balanced," I said. "I'm not sure this is safe."

"Relax," Rosemary urged me. "I've got you. Relax," she said. "I'm not going to let go."

And I did.

I let myself fall limp in her arms and forgot about the danger all around us, the perilous height, the squirmy water moccasins, the lightning storm that was no doubt boiling up somewhere nearby. I relaxed and looked, as Rosemary had insisted, at the water, which was dyed like a volcanic rainbow from the horizon line to just in front of my eyes. In some spots, it was so red it suggested a valentine heart, slick with the leavings of a kiss. In other spots, at the base of some tiny waves, the blackness was as complete as the oil these derricks once methodically sucked up from the earth's heart. I relaxed and leaned back into Rosemary as she leaned against a sturdy iron leg. I closed my eyes and saw that sunset dance on the inside of my eyelids. I relaxed and breathed deep, felt my heartbeat slow, rose and fell like a life raft on Rosemary's chest as it rose and fell, our breaths aligning themselves until like a single person we sat on top of the derrick in the waning light, sighing and eyeing the day's brilliant end.

When we finally climbed down into the canoe, the sun had almost completely disappeared: only a band of neon crimson marked the horizon, like a racing stripe. The bullfrogs, a legion of tireless sousaphones, began to choir and splash amongst the whistling reeds. "Can we find our way to shore?" Rosemary asked. "Is there enough light?"

"I think so," I said.

"I bet the canoe man has left," Rosemary suggested. "I bet he's gone home to his wife and kids."

"I paid in advance," I told her. "And he said we could just leave the canoe next to the others if he wasn't there when we got back."

"What if somebody steals it?"

"I don't think he's worried about that," I said, although it would certainly be easy enough for some teenagers with a pickup to haul the thing away.

"You know," Rosemary said, "I think we should do this a lot more."

"Uh-huh."

"Definitely every year on this day," she said. "An anniversary canoe trip. Every year."

My paddle thumped against the canoe. "As long as I'm around," I said, knowing even as I said it that it was the wrong thing to say, but having no way to take it back without it sounding even worse than it already was.

Rosemary was silent for a minute or two. She paddled hard. So hard that I was forced to steer more than paddle. "Well, of course," she finally managed, and I could hear the hurt and anger in her voice. "Every year until you're gone. Of course."

"Mrs. Lemon called," my mother said when I got home from school and wandered into the kitchen to get a snack. "The prosthetic lady," she clarified unnecessarily; scarcely a moment passed in the day or night that I didn't think about Delia Lemon's fingers, her warm, soft palm against my face. "She said your hand is ready. Your hook, that is. And we can come pick it up anytime."

"Tomorrow," I said.

"Well. No. By the time you get home from school and we get over there, they'll be closed. I was thinking we might go on Saturday. She said it would take a while to explain how everything worked and you might want to spend some time there getting used to it, making any necessary adjustments." My mother turned back to the kitchen counter, where she was rolling chicken parts in flour for frying. "I was thinking I might drop you off—I'd come in with you for a few minutes, of course—and then go to the mall to get my Christmas shopping done. If you promise to behave yourself, that is."

My mind was reeling with images of a long afternoon spent in the back room of Lemon's Prosthetics. I imagined Delia and myself sprawled on a bed that was mysteriously, inexplicably there, if only in my mind, her manicured nails running up and down the inside of my arm, her breath in my ear, her lips pressed hard against my own.

"Could you? Behave yourself?" my mother asked.

I fumbled. "What? I don't know what you're—"

"If I go Christmas shopping. Promise not to get in the bags while I'm driving home? I don't want you to ruin any surprises."

I smiled at my mother's back. The grease in the frying pan popped and hissed. "Scout's honor," I said, raising my stump as witness.

"I've been thinking about Rosemary," Brautigan says at our next meeting.

"You and me both," I say.

"And I have to admit I'm a little concerned about something. A little confused."

I begin to feel uncomfortable. Brautigan has been a wonderful ear in regard to Rosemary. He has listened and kept his mouth shut, grunting at the right times, knitting his eyebrows when appropriate. I feel my stomach churn a bit, afraid that Brautigan is finally going to say, "Enough!" and declare my obsession ridiculous. I fear he's going to chide me, to stop humoring me and insist that I "move on." I resettle myself on my seat, clear my throat, try to make myself sound as normal as possible. "What?" I say.

"I'm not entirely convinced she's who she says she is."

"I beg your pardon?" His suggestion sounds like a line from some ridiculous old movie, one packed full of private eyes, femmes fatales, fat villains, and simpering stool pigeons.

"I don't fully believe that she is the actual Kentucky Fried Rat Lady. It seems to me that, while her history is certainly tragic, it really, except for the rats and the chicken, has very little to do with the KFRat legend.

For one thing, she was eating the chicken at home. There was no family involved. And the chicken was a chicken, not a rat." Brautigan stops to nod at me, as if his bobbing head will convince me he is right, even if his words should fall short. "The fact is, your Rosemary suffered horribly. The true story is so much more gruesome than the legend, I'm not convinced the two are connected at all. Legends usually exaggerate things, make them bigger and more exciting. In her case, if Rosemary is the basis for the legend, the circumstances have been altered so that the legend is *less* gruesome. The rumor mill has minimized the trauma, sanitized it for public consumption. Does Rosemary have any proof that she is the real live victim upon whom the Rat Lady is modeled? Is her name mentioned in any newspaper articles, scholarly reports?"

I am shaken. "Well. No. I don't think so. But I don't know why she would make something like that up."

"Yes," Brautigan agrees. "But delusions of grandeur are rarely easily explained. Why would someone choose to believe themselves Napoleon when they might just as easily be Buddha or Hank Aaron? Catherine the Great? Nefertiti?"

"So, you're suggesting Rosemary was—is—mentally unbalanced?" I begin to get a little angry.

"Well. No. Just. Mistaken." Brautigan smiles at me.

I lean forward in my chair. "Look, pal, if you think I'm going to sit here and let you insult and psychoanalyze my friends—who aren't even present to defend themselves—then you're . . . well, you're not even a therapist or analyst or anything. You're a folklorist, remember?"

"And you're a folkloric character."

"I'm a person. And so is Rosemary."

"Right. She's a person who thinks she's a folkloric character."

"Well, so am I."

"No. You *are* a folkloric character. You're the genuine article. I'll certify that. Rosemary only *thinks* she's a folkloric character. That doesn't make her any less of a person. Or a crazy. It just makes her of little real use to my studies. In terms of the Kentucky Fried Rat story. She's still useful in terms of you, though. In terms of how she affected you. Since you left Wichita Falls for Florida, how many times have you struck? Not counting the time you took me with you."

"Um," I say, doing the math in my head, although there is no real math to be done. "Um. None. I haven't struck once. Since then."

"Since the last time you saw Rosemary. Since you fled and she moved and the two of you have been out of touch. Not once?"

I sink back in my chair, uncertain if I should feel ashamed or cured. "No. Not once."

My brother and I stood awestruck beneath the flapping canvas posters, ashamed for our curiosity but unable to move. GONGA THE GIRL-RILLA, QUEEN OF THE APE-WOMEN! hovered above us, her announcing letters choked with jungle vines. The cartoon figure, a gorilla with supermodel breasts and an angel's face, stamped the ground beneath her ferociously. To her left, a neon-bright poster touted the creepy courage of TARSEM!, who slept, ate and danced in a viper pit, cuddling needle-toothed pythons like teddy bears, like feather boas plucked and soaked in venom. Next to those dangerous curlicues, hateful s's, the poster my brother and I looked at only on the sly, catching firefly glimpses, blinking at the atrocity painted there in horrific detail: LEON THE HUMAN TRUNK! Sans arms and legs, stumps recalling my own singular, still-healing misfortune, he smiled down at us like a Thalidomide Jesu, blissful, at peace with his unlucky lot in this incarnation. Though we both itched to pay the exorbitant price required to allow one an audience with these and countless other FREAKS! (The banner "said" that word like a prospector might shriek *Eureka!*), we fought the urge valiantly, commenting now and again on the number of corny dogs that might be purchased instead for the same shameful dollars.

"Hey," a boy my age said, coming up to where we stood admiring GONGA's gargantuan nipples. "Hey," he said, quite honestly, without a bit of meanness in his voice, "are you part of the show? Hey, are you? One of the freaks?" He pointed up and over at LEON. "Is that you? You LEON?"

In the last few blocks, I'd begun to develop butterflies in my gut. Sweat, despite the excess dose of deodorant I'd applied that morning, trickled down my sides. My mother, upon first sealing herself in the truck's cab with me, had sniffed a bit, but didn't comment on the deluge of cologne I'd slathered upon myself. (I had planned an excuse in the event she did say something: "That Lemon lady wears so much perfume, this is the only way I can stand to be that close to her.") Once on Main Street, I was near frantic with desire.

"It'll feel weird at first, I imagine," my mother said. "But don't fight

Mrs. Lemon. Just let her tell you what to do, and you'll get used to it in no time."

We pulled up in front of Lemon's Prosthetics, and I was out of the door before my mother had put the car fully in park. "Calm down!" she said, but I scarcely heard her over the sound of my slamming door and roiling hormones. If all went right, my mother would stay for a minute or two—no more than that, surely—and then it would be just me and Delia, alone and unencumbered.

I stopped before opening the door, drew a deep breath and suppressed—or tried to, at least—my grin. "Think 'suave,' " I reminded myself.

"Can I help you?" the man behind the counter asked.

I didn't say anything, but looked behind him for Delia. She was nowhere to be seen.

"Can I help you?" the man repeated, raising his voice a couple of decibels.

My mother came in behind me. "Yes," she said. "We're here about his prosthesis. We have an appointment, but we're a little early."

I could stand it no longer. "Where's Delia?" I demanded.

The man cocked his head and wrinkled his brow. "My wife? She's not working today." My hopes fell in shambles. "But I can take care of you, no problem." He came out from behind the counter to shake my hand. He was wearing shorts, making it easy to see that his left leg was made of plastic and metal joints. His grip was firm, practiced, intimidating. "We'll have you fixed up chop-chop."

*   *   *

I turn Rusty's infernal crypto-log over and over, like a pig on a spit, like a player piano's spooled tunes. I read it backward and forward, diagonally, like a crossword puzzle. I rearrange letters to make new words, copy the sequence on paper again and again, omitting all but the capital letters in one instance. I go to the library and check out books on cryptography, soak the whole damned thing in lemon juice and hold it close to the flames of my gas stove. I buy a black-light bulb and try to read the log in its spooky purple glow. I sleep with it near my bed, hoping those last moments before slumber will surprise me with a new idea. I blindfold myself and feel the grooves and knots and scarified letters with my good hand, hoping for a trace of Braille. I consider having a bonfire and tossing the log in, standing close over it to sniff its smoldering secrets. I hate it for its apparent meaning-lessness and despise myself for my inability to crack its code.

I don't know exactly what the JOLLY ROGER FOLLIES were, a play, a musical, operetta or evening of vaudevillian antics. I scoured the box, digging through eye patches and hoop earrings, crumpled swords and broken spy scopes, looking for a program or flyer or copy of the script. But there was nothing. Nothing but the cheap costumes and props and incredible, impossible, real pirate hook was left of the FOLLIES.

That afternoon, when I got home, I dug through my mother's ad-dress book until I found the phone number of Lemon's Prosthetics. I hadn't been back in years, hadn't seen Delia Lemon since the time she'd touched my face and told me I was handsome and desirable. Each time, every two years or so, I'd gone back for adjustments on the

straps that went from my hook up around my shoulder blades, Mr.
Lemon and his strong arms and sexy fake leg had been in the office
alone, and he greeted me as a fishing buddy, regaling me with tales of
fantastic prosthetics he'd fitted on amputees in the space of time since
last we'd met. I'd given up on seeing Delia again, convinced myself
that she was a figment of my imagination, her voice and touch made
more smooth and erotic by my mind's unstoppable tendency toward
romanticism. I thought now that I might take the pirate hook to
Lemon's and let Mr. Lemon (he forever first-nameless) see it, adjust
the leather straps and rawhide laces so it would be not just wearable
but comfortable.

"Hello. Lemon's Prosthetics," she answered after two rings. She—
of course, she: Delia Lemon—still sounding as throaty and exotic as
she did years ago, when I was so overwhelmed by the concept of sex
and my proximity to its possible occurrence I fairly swooned.

"Hi," I said. "I'm a client, and I was wondering if maybe you'd have
time to see me about a new prosthetic I'm interested in. I found it in
a box of pirate stuff."

I go home to a mailbox bursting with magazines and nothing else. No
bills, flyers, ads, postcards, letters. I carefully rip all the perfume strips
out and walk to the closet to deposit them. When I open the door, I
realize things have gotten way out of hand. The accumulated strips, a
fragrant tower of paper grown wild out of its box, leans, lurches, tumbles outward, onto me, all over me, knocking me to the ground like a
dim-witted cartoon character opening a closet full of water. I am

swimming in odors, my eyes watering from fumes, brain reeling from olfactory overload. As if in the grip of some religious experience, I am suddenly transported back to a last afternoon with Rosemary—a picnic—and the smell of her hair and skin, talcum powder, perfume, honeysuckle, grass, mustard on the sandwiches, watermelon sugar, beer, sun, wind, earth. Over that cinematic memory, a soundtrack plays. Our last conversation:

"Love is not a monster," Rosemary is saying, angrily. "It's not. Yes, it creeps up on you and pounces, but you don't have to shriek and run away from it."

"Or drive off, tires squealing," I add, recognizing the scene all too well.

Rosemary: "If they didn't drive off, what would you do?"

"I don't know. Talk to them, I guess."

"And they'd realize that you are the nicest guy in the world, Leonard. They'd probably fall in love with you. Like I have. Like I am." She wraps her arms around me and squeezes.

I didn't know what else to do but squeeze back. So I did.

But I was not the monster at hand. It was something else. And in the end, I sped away like a scared kid, heart racing, head spinning. Leaving Rosemary by herself, forced to contend with the monster alone, in the dark, miles from civilization.

"Good afternoon," Delia said when I came into the store. I'd parked the truck in the same spot I always did, a space that mysteriously seemed to be reserved for me.

She stepped from behind the counter.

I had prepared myself, of course, to be disappointed. I had told myself—aloud even—during the drive over that I was certain to find her far removed from the vision I'd first encountered and had subsequently dreamed of as the ideal for so many years.

But I was wrong. She seemed unchanged, as if she herself were wholly synthetic, emerging every half-decade or so from a crate hidden deep within Lemon's Prosthetics' warehouse of arms, legs, feet, eyes, God only knew what else. If when we'd first met she seemed to be no more than twenty-three, she appeared now to be not a day older. Whereas I, in uncharitable spurts and countless grueling metamorphoses, had changed dramatically. I was hardly the same person. I doubted Delia could recognize me, but could not find the power of speech anywhere in my head to announce my identity, to reintroduce myself and make small talk, chatter. As a last resort at communication before turning tail to flee, I held the pirate hook up in front of my noisy heart.

"Come with me," Delia said, moving toward the back offices where her husband and I had spent so many painful afternoons, testing the strength of new cables and stiff leather. "Let's see what we can do."

When Brautigan doesn't appear for our Friday appointment, I decide to nix waiting around or searching for him and take a walk instead. I head south on the road going out to the Railroad Tracks and car-pushing Dead Kids. Next to the abandoned rock shop, a group of students in a Jeep pass, honking and waving. I don't imagine they're going out to try their luck with the ghost kids, not at noon, so maybe the road *does* go somewhere, out to the Rio or some secret green canyon. A sign on the rock shop door says, "Gone fishing for good." I look in the window, where all is, as you might expect, dark and dusty. It was a bad idea from the get-go, this place. Who needs rocks here? Not a big tourist town, Alpine, and one need only bend down to pick up a rock for free. On a whim I try the door, which opens smoothly, without the requisite haunted-house creak. "Hello?" I say.

There is no echo, no scurry of mice or bats or sharp-beaked goblins. No transient has taken to using the place as bedroom. No kids have broken in to smash glass cases or spell out foul words in amber and geodes. It is museum-quality quiet and, excepting the dust, neat.

I pick up a piece of petrified wood off a table marked "Final Clearance," and consider its heft in my hand. If one subscribes to a postmodern philosophy, it is reasonable to believe that some of the tree this wood came from did not petrify. It rotted, and each atom went its own way, taking up residence in the earth, joining a group of likeminded atoms intent on forming a truffle, potato or orchid, being gobbled by a gopher, perhaps a sniffling aardvark. All the other atoms moved on, made something of themselves, went with the flow, rolled with the punches, changed with the times. But not these atoms. These atoms are stuck. These atoms are going nowhere fast.

"I don't know," I say out loud. And I shock myself, because I don't know what I mean by that. I don't know what?

And then it hits me. I'm re-answering Rosemary's question about what I would do if I caught the parkers I stalk. I don't know, I told her. Talk to them, I guess, I said.

What would I do?

I would not bust a window, headlight or windshield with my hook while uttering some witty movie-bad-guy one-liner.

I would not slash, stab or strangle.

I would not chase them away on foot, then come back and take the car.

I would not torture them mentally, emotionally or physically.

I would not, at any point, laugh maniacally.

I would not sneer lecherously.

I would not bite the head off a passing dove.

I would not quote liberally from *Richard III*.

I would not metamorphose into a wolf, demon or bloodthirsty Venusian.

I would not make my eyes glow hypnotically, my canines extend abnormally or my nails turn clawlike.

In truth, I don't know what I would do.

Maybe I would ask for a ride back to town.

Or maybe I'd say, "Oh, sorry. I thought you were somebody else." Maybe that's what I'd do.

I try it out. "Sorry," I say out loud. "Sorry," I say to the petrified wood. "I thought you were somebody else."

Brautigan drives me over to look at the Marfa Ghost. Lights. I've been here before, on my own. We stand in front of the historical marker, reading silently, then move, like mirror images, away from it, behind it, into the dark expanse where the Lights dance and glow wildly, daring people to explain their existence and simultaneously disbelieve all offered explanations. (Frankly, there's an article framed and posted in the lobby of the Marfa Waldorf that concludes scientifically and undisputably the Lights are nothing more than ordinary headlights from many miles away, distorted and transported to the empty desert by the earth's curvature and some curiously intense heat waves rising off the sun-baked sands. The Hotel staff doesn't acknowledge the article and will not point it out to curious visitors eager to buy an I SAW THE LIGHTS bumper sticker. Only the most determined and unlucky tourist happens upon the truth, time-faded and half hidden behind a dusty potted palm. Woe unto him or her. I myself have struggled mightily to shake the teeth of science from my need to believe the Lights are something more than the product of Ford or Chevrolet.)

"I'm going to take a semester's sabbatical," Brautigan says to me and the darkness. He stands with his hands in his pockets, somewhat adrift without the comforting weight and mass of his pad and pen.

"A vacation," I say, calling it what it is.

"Partly. I'm compiling a book of legends concerning the Los Angeles sewers."

"What about them?"

"Oh, about the things that people think are down there. Animals, people, potent varieties of albino marijuana."

The Lights blink and change colors like a Christmas display viewed from across two football fields.

"Well, be careful," I caution.

"Oh, yeah. I will be."

On the highway behind us a pickup whizzes past without slowing.

"Does this have anything to do with your newfound habit? The lurking thing? Think L.A. will deter you?"

"No, no," Brautigan says. "I've been meaning to do some work on this project for quite a while. Started it in grad school and never got back to it." He hums for a moment or two before asking me, "Will you be here when I get back? Maybe we could finish up then."

"Yes," I say. "Barring miracles and catastrophes, I'll be here a long time." I think of Rusty and DeeDee's mystery log in my living room, imagine my mail carrier at home, dozing in front of the television, resting up for tomorrow. "A long, long time." I hold my good hand up in front of my eyes and try to catch a Light in the silhouette of my trembling grip. It scoots away over and over, as if aware of my long-range safari, impervious to capture. "I'll be here until further notice," I say.

PART | TWO

PART TWO

We're driving—Brautigan and me—to El Paso. North on 118. It's mid-afternoon, the sun high above us, out of sight; we may as well be lit by overhead bulbs. The landscape we traverse is monumental, but widespread. On either side of us, an indistinguishable distance away, mountains run like cutouts, like a dentist's nightmare of an alligator's bottom jaw, perpetually open, forever aahing. There is nothing about the mountains that marks one from another. None is so much higher than the others that it stands out. None is shaped so much more like a crowing rooster or rutting elephants that it deserves its own name and postcard. (Rusty would be devastated.) The way they run beside us, they may as well be on a giant revolving canvas being pedaled by a Cyclops to match Brautigan's desperate speed. The valley floor we cross is as desolate as any planet visited by any astronaut on any given episode of *The Twilight Zone* or *The Outer Limits*. With the exception of a charred gas station every forty miles or so, and the phone and power lines, the very road we're on, there is no evidence humans have ever passed this way before. Indeed, we've seen only a few farm vehicles, ancient chugging Dodge trucks and Ford flatbeds, during our quest. Their drivers dutifully raised a left hand from the top of the steering wheel to acknowledge our momentary presence. Faces flash by so quickly it's difficult to determine their sex, much less their demeanor. "At night," Brautigan says, pointing left with his right hand, "if you drive this road at night, those saguaros look like people sometimes, off to the side of the road, hitchhiking or just standing there. And once, my wife almost hit a panther."

I raise my eyebrows.

Brautigan shrugs. "Well, she said it was a panther."

Brautigan and I said our good-byes over the phone last night. He planned to be off to Los Angeles in the morning, alone but for his tape recorder and notepads. I was far behind on my reading; a stack of magazines the size of a sofa awaited my attention, and I'd just put on a pot of coffee when my doorbell rang. I halfway expected it to be the UPS man bringing another crazy offering for DeeDee, a stained-glass atlas or toothpick log cabin, each tiny sliver whittled with algebraic equations. "Who is it?" I asked the chained door.

"They got him," Brautigan exclaimed, breathless.

"Is that you?"

"Did you hear me? They got him."

"I thought you were leaving at dawn?"

Brautigan pounded his fist against the door three times. "God-damnit, open up. They got him. In El Paso."

I unlatched the chain and opened the door. "What in the hell are you talking about?"

"The Axe Man. Remember? Your evil counterpart? Hangs out in mall parking lots, stows away in station wagons dressed up like a little old lady. Sits on his axe to hide it. They caught him. In El Paso. Outside a Service Merchandise. He mistakenly took refuge in a Marine recruiting officer's Chevette. Sergeant Slaughter came out with a new wok and wasn't having any of the granny-in-distress act. Veteran of too many drag queen come-ons in port-of-call bars. Coldcocked him, the bad guy, the faux little old lady from Pasadena. The Axe Man cometh to in jail, and he's going to sing."

I noticed that Brautigan had his bags with him. "What's with the luggage?"

Sighing, he barged past me, heading for the kitchen and the smell of coffee, suitcases slapping against his legs like saddlebags. "I went by my office on the way to the airport, had to pick up a couple of journals, and there was a message from a friend of mine who works at the *El Paso Beacon*. So I came straight here." He looked down at his bags, dropped them on the floor at his side. "I don't know why I brought the suitcases in. I could have left them in the car, I suppose."

"The trip's off?"

"The trip's different. We're going to El Paso." He rummaged around in my cupboards until he found the cabinet with the coffee mugs and pulled out an official souvenir of Beavers Bend State Park, Oklahoma.

"What do you mean 'we'?"

Brautigan dragged a chair back from my kitchen table and sat down. "How long would it take you to get ready?"

"Ready for what?" I was becoming perturbed, not yet having had my own coffee, brushed my teeth or used the john. The linoleum floor was cold against my bare feet.

Brautigan reached for the packets of sugar I keep in a bowl in the center of my table, took four, doused his coffee liberally. "To go. To El Paso. To interview him."

I was uncertain how Brautigan expected me to react; I myself didn't know how to respond. It would have surprised me less if my dead father, wielding a harp and my long-ago-buried hand, had materialized on my doorstep in a flutter of angel's wings, announcing the arrival of Armageddon. I was, it's true, glad to see Brautigan; the thought of being without his ear and shoulder and friendship had weighed heavily on my mind since he first announced his sudden leave-taking. I was also a little jealous; he felt no guilt in abandoning me in Alpine to pursue another folkloric interest, and now that another exotic urban-legendary character had appeared, he dropped everything for him. In addition, I was a tad sickened, knowing nothing of the Axe Man but what Brautigan's students talked about in class that day several weeks ago. My connection to this criminal, tenuous as it is, leaves me feeling a little slimy; Brautigan had no problem linking us in that class, and the fact that the students chose to examine the Axe Man and myself in tandem suggests that we may be, despite the huge differences between our exploits, lumped together in the mass psyche. (I must reiterate here that I have never had occasion to be picked up even for questioning by the authorities. The Axe Man's police record lies somewhere closer to Brautigan's than my own.) "I don't know," I told Brautigan, "that I want to be or should be a part of this particular expedition. I mean, the Dead-Kids-at-the-Railroad-Tracks outing was one thing, but this seems a little crazy."

Brautigan blew on his coffee and frowned. "Crazy? How?"

"I mean, you're the doctor. The researcher. I'm just the Hook Man."

"Bushwa! If anybody should be in on the ground floor of this one, it's you." He sipped at the rim of his cup. "Come on," he whined. "Don't make me go alone."

My jealousy and anger flared a bit, brought out of hiding by Brautigan's admission that he wanted me around. I had the upper hand. "You certainly didn't have a problem going to Los Angeles alone," I sniped. "I thought you were through with my 'project' for the time being. I thought I was 'on ice.' "

Brautigan put his mug down and looked at me, eyes wide and brimming with honesty, like a spy or a lover challenged to test his loyalty to the cause. "I was wrong," he said. "I was leaving for all the wrong reasons. We can talk about them in the car, if you feel the need. But the fact of the matter is, fate or destiny or coincidence has dropped this guy in our laps, and we would be fools to ignore the opportunity we have. Yes, 'we,' " he said, holding my gaze like Rasputin charming the czarina to de-panty in the wine cellar. "You know as well as I do that this project stopped being 'mine' some time ago. It's about us now. I'm not suggesting we continue in order to discover some vaccine to save ourselves or those who follow us, but that we delve deeper into your story and my story and his story in order to understand. It's not a lot to ask, I don't think.

"Listen," he said, and for an instant I thought he was going to reach out to take my hand or my hook. "I need you. With me. In El Paso. We're not talking about a fucking exorcism here. An interview or two, that's all." He picked his mug up and raised it to his lips. "That's all," he said.

"Can I have some time to think about this?" I asked.

"No. I'm going to go gas up the car, tell the wife the change in plans and dash by the library to check a fact or two. I'll be back in two hours to pick you up." He stood. "Do you have a paper cup or something so I can take this with me?" he said, indicating his coffee.

I went to the cabinet and pulled out a plastic tumbler emblazoned with Darth Vader's face, faded now to an almost invisible gray after many years of washing.

"Something smaller?" Brautigan asked, but I shook my head no and he took it. Holding it in his teeth by its edge, he stooped for his suitcases and headed for the door. Before it shut behind him, I heard him grunt and assumed he was saying again that he would be back in two hours.

He knew me. Knew what my decision would be.

I went to my room to begin packing.

What does one pack for an expedition to confront a maniac, one penned like a chicken-eating cur or a tiger with a taste for tender, cooing babies? Clothes, yes, but how many shirts? Pairs of pants?

Socks, underwear, T-shirts? Is it a formal occasion, sucking the marrow of truth horrifique from the blood-lozenged mouth of a cross-dressing madman? Does one need a jacket, a tie? An ascot, cummerbund, boutonniere? Am I expected to look like myself, or like Dr. Brautigan's equal, his assistant? What does a witness for the inquisition wear?

I opened my closet to find an infestation of flannel and denim.

Is it an insult to dress like a lumberjack (albeit one whose career has already been cut short not by Axe! or Chainsaw! but lawnmower) on an occasion such as this? I thought back to what Brautigan wore the first time we got down to business: chambray shirt, pressed khaki slacks, a tie so colorful it appeared to be a crevasse leading into a cartoon world. It seemed, his outfit, appropriate then. Official, but not overwhelmingly so. He looked comfortable, and in appearing so he put me at ease.

"I don't," I told my closet, "have a thing to wear."

And so I found myself jogging down to what passes in Alpine for a department store.

Moving quickly from department to department, each the size of a closet, Wissler's being absurdly tiny, I picked out a pair of trousers, a plastic-packaged button-down white dress shirt and a tie featuring paisleys that hunted each other's squiggly tails like amoebas on vacation, on the make, in pursuit of love. "Job interview?" A young girl walked up behind me as I made my second tie selection. HEATHER, her name tag read.

"What?"

"You must have a job interview. You're getting all spruced up."

"No, actually," I said, "I'm just, um, going away and need to look nice."

"Oh," Heather moaned, smiling. "I just got some new clothes. For interviewing. And graduation." She took the shirt out of my hands and held a blue-and-green-striped tie in front of it. "That looks nice," she said, turning to look at me, gauging my reaction to her creation. The stripes were obscenely wide.

I felt myself blushing, needing to get out of here as quickly as possible.

"Are you graduating? Are you going somewhere for a graduation trip?"

"I'm sorry," I said. "Am I graduating?"

Heather put down the green-and-blue tie and picked up a red one with cherry-sized white polka dots. "Right. Are you?"

"No," I admitted. "I'm not."

"I was just wondering. What do you think of this one? This red, I think, is nice. It's like clown's hair, you know. It says, 'Hello!' "

"Right," I said. " 'Hello!' "

"So, you've got, what? Another semester? Then you'll start shopping for interviews."

I was trying to keep up. I really was. But I was not sure we were involved in the same conversation. "I like that tie," I said, reaching out to touch one of the polar-bear-white dots. When my finger touched the silk, I suddenly remembered the hook, tried to shift the packages it held to disguise its pointy nature. It was, for the first time in so many years, an embarrassment.

"Yeah. You know what it reminds me of? That Beatles movie. *Yellow Submarine*? Remember when they get lost in that land of holes with Jeremy the Nowhere Man? The guy they sing 'Nowhere Man' to? And then at the end, when the cartoon stops and the real Beatles are on-screen? And Paul—or maybe it's George, I'm not sure—says, 'I've got a 'ole in me pocket.' " Heather paused to breathe. "That's what this tie reminds me of a little bit. So, what'd you do your paper on?"

"What paper?"

"For Brautigan." She saw that I didn't get her and continued: "I'm in your class. Folklore. I know I've seen you in there. So what'd you do your paper on? I did the 'Mexican Pet' thing. About the giant wharf rat that eats the two girls' little dog. Or cat, depending on who tells it."

"I," I said, "didn't do a paper."

Heather looks at me like I just admitted to shooting Kennedy.

"I didn't have to."

"Oh," Heather drawled. "You were auditing." She held the polka-dot tie up against the shirt again. "You have to get this one. I think red is your color."

I'd never thought of myself as having a color, but I was flattered to think that Heather would have such an opinion, assuming that she wasn't just trying to sell a tie. "Yes," I said, "I'll take it."

"You know." Heather sighed. She took the cuff of my shirt and began to pull me into the next department. It was the first time a woman had touched me since the night before Rosemary and I said our farewells. The feel of her fingernails touching me through the flannel around my wrist literally shocked me, but in a most pleasant way.

It was like being hypnotized. She pulled me along after her, and I could do nought but follow. I was in her command. So much so that she could say practically anything without my balking or disagreeing or even thinking. "You know," she said again, "I couldn't believe how cool it was of you to sit through that whole Hook Man debate/presentation thing. You must have been really itching to get in on it. I mean, it's like, everybody was so intent on generalizing. I mean, I saw you back there and I wanted to say, 'Hey, everybody. Clue in. It's like telling racist jokes right in front of somebody who's, you know, part of that race. The one being made fun of. But then, I thought, no, he's probably getting off on this because he's probably doing his paper on Hook Man and this is the best kind of research possible. I mean, if you had to do a paper, you'd have to pick Hook Man, right? You've got the inside scoop."

"What?" I said, coming out of my trance for a moment.

And then we were waltzing past the perfume and cologne counter, and I was flabbergasted. I stopped, shocked by the scents that fell upon me like campfire smoke, amazed at the sight of bottle after bottle caged like statuesque tarantulas in glass cases. My sleeve slipped out of Heather's grip. I felt on the verge of swooning—my father's cologne, late summer hay, Rosemary's neck, grass, just cut, still pungent, green, my closet, persimmons at midnight—when Heather retraced the two steps she'd taken away from me, lightly took hold of my cuff again and pulled me after her, out of the dangerous zone of aromas.

"I want to show you these great shoes," Heather said. "They just came in day before yesterday, and they are very, very you."

*   *   *

"You. Do. Some-thing to me. Some-thing that simp-ly mys-ti-fies me," Rosemary sang. She was sitting on the ground next to her porch, pulling weeds out from between the sunflowers that were just beginning to sprout. "Look," she said, looking up at me. "Look at this." She held a tiny stone up close to her eyes, then, smiling, rose and carried it to me on the glider. I put down my *Harper's* and leaned forward. "Look," Rosemary said. "It's a heart. It's a fossilized heart."

I held my hand out, and she placed it gingerly in the center of my palm, as if it were something delicate, still alive, not a sea urchin dead many thousands of years.

"It's beautiful," Rosemary said. She reached out and brushed it gently, petted it where it lay just below my own heart line. "It's a fossilized heart," Rosemary said. "Isn't it?" She looked up at me, her lips turned upward into the faintest smile.

The drive-in wouldn't begin to fill with cars for another hour or so. I could hear the concession stand workers beginning to get started. The first kernels of popcorn popped, echoed like tiny gunshots.

"Yes," I lied. "It is."

"I think it's great, somebody your age coming back to college to get their degree," Heather cooed. "Not that you're old or anything." She began to ring up the purchases I'd selected, including a belt she insisted I buy and a pair of suede bucks that I "couldn't possibly live without."

"I mean, my dad, he didn't finish his degree. Mom got pregnant, and he had to get a serious job. But he's always regretted it." Heather held the polka-dot tie up against the white shirt yet again and nodded her head. "I mean not finishing the degree. Not Mom getting pregnant. He doesn't regret that. I guess. That was my oldest brother, and he's kind of a loser, so maybe he does. I don't know." She shrugged. "My point is, just because you're older than everybody else on campus, the students, I mean, doesn't mean that you should feel weird or out of place or anything. I mean, there are lots of professors a lot older than you running around, and they fit in fine."

"I like campus," I said, and it was the truth. I meant it.

Heather finished entering the prices. Before she hit the total button, she put her hands on her hips and frowned at me. "But I never see you around. You should hang out more." She turned, hit the total button, then, seeing my credit card out of the corner of her eye, took it and ran it through the security check. When she handed it back to me, she held it tight so I had to pull to get it away from her. "When you get back from your mysterious trip, we should get a beer sometime." She winked at me. "Really. You could wear your new clothes."

Dear Sir: (Dr. Brautigan's letter in response to my letter regarding his article began)

I am, as you might imagine, genuinely intrigued by your claim. Would you be interested in meeting with me? I can be reached by phone through my departmental office. Call collect.

Sincerely,
Peter Brautigan, Ph.D.

PS: Where were you on the night of October 22nd? (A joke.)

"Come on, come on!" Brautigan hollered at me when he saw me. He leaned against the door of his car, hands clutching a map. My Darth Vader cup sat on the roof of the car, as if reading over his shoulder. "Let's go!" he insisted, superheroesque.

"I'm almost finished packing," I told him. "I had to run to the store to pick up a few things."

"Christ. You think they don't have stores in El Paso?"

"Hold your horses." I went inside and stuck the Wissler's bag in my half-empty suitcase, filling it. And then, seized by the urge, I put Rusty's rock and log in a duffel bag awarded to me by the people responsible for *Sports Illustrated*. Lugging my suitcase and the weighty duffel outside, I locked the door and, turning, noticed that my mailbox hung a tad loose from its wall mount.

"We can't go," I announce.

"What?"

"We can't go. Yet. We have to do an errand."

The Alpine post office, a square apple on an ocean of limeade grass, looks from the outside like a property designed and maintained by the Walt Disney Company. Inside, its very air is stained brown with the smell of paper and time. A mural spanning the wall above the teller windows shows clouds like cotton balls suspended over a valley of mesquite and Rorshachian cattle. A bulletin board, like a magnet for flyers, hangs in shadow next to a desk where boys turning eighteen can fill out a form committing themselves to a supporting role in any

upcoming military adventures. WANTED WANTED WANTED, the bulletin board's posters screech over scowling murderers' grimy fore-
heads, evil fingerprints. I WANT YOU, Uncle Sam lusts in bold serif
type, his finger almost three-dimensional, coming at me like the claws
of Vincent Price in *House of Wax*. "Want something?" the teller said to
me between high-pitched hiccups.

"I need," I announced, "to have my mail held. I'm leaving town."

The teller raised his caterpillarish eyebrows. "Are you now?" he
said, leaning forward to inspect my face closely. "I'll be right back."
He spun and disappeared behind a screen that masked, I imagine, a
workroom of drug-slowed octogenarians bungling their way through
the day's delivery piles.

What did that mean? "I'll be right back"? Where the hell was he
going? Did I need special permission to leave town? Was a notary public required?

REMEMBER, a sign behind the counter cautioned, MAIL THEFT
IS A FEDERAL OFFENSE.

Someone passed close behind the screen. I heard the jangle of keys
on a belt. Possibly handcuffs?

There was a long silence.

Then scuffling feet, and a face peeped around the screen to gawk
at me a moment. It withdrew suddenly, like a spook-house phantom
awaiting its next carnival victim.

What is this? A sting operation? I pictured Rusty's postcards sitting
in a drawer in my kitchen, secreted beneath a tray of silver. His words,
trapped under a pile of tines and dented soup spoons, echoed in my
head.

The teller, returning, hiccupped thrice. "Now don't you go any-where," he told me before returning again to whatever limbo the screen camouflaged. "Hurry," I heard him hiss at a cohort. "Hurry, damnit, before he leaves."

Slowly, like a virgin suddenly aware that she's stumbled into a coven of black-hearted witches, I began to walk backward toward the door. Adrenaline pumping, I became hyperaware; I heard a clock tick-ing; an air conditioner rumbled to life above my head, animating the bulletin board's thumbtacked gallery. When my back touched the glass doors, I turned and pushed, walked briskly to the Volkswagen and, sliding in, commanded, "Drive."

"Do you know a girl in your class named Heather?" I ask Brautigan.

"Who? Heather?" He drums his fingers in contagion against the gear-shift knob. "No. Why?"

"She did her paper on some killer rat or something."

"The Mexican Pet. I remember five papers on the Mexican Pet. Heather." He runs the name through his memory and out his mouth. "Heather. Heather. Heather. Mexican girl?"

"No."

"Heather. Heather. Heather." Brautigan looks at me and shrugs. "Survey classes. Too damned big. Why? Do you know her?"

"Yes," I say, then reconsider. "No. I just met her. She helped me at Wissler's." There's a long pause that requires me to continue. "She was very helpful."

"Heather. Heather. Heather." Brautigan chants the name like a mantra.

"Heather. Heather. Heather." I join him.

We leave Alpine behind us, moaning the name like an incantation, a spell we're casting. Except we don't know what it is we want, what it is we're conjuring, what desperate magic rises up in our wake.

"Who are you?"

"What?"

"Who," I correct. "Tell me who you are."

Rosemary and I were sitting—for the first time—on her delicious glider. We'd had dinner at the Waffle House, again, and she'd asked me back, enticing me with a promise of homemade ice cream riddled with Butterfinger crumbs.

"I'm just me," she said, laughing. In retrospect, I think I can find some discomfort in that laughter. "I'm nobody special," she lied.

"Who are you?"

"What?"

"Who," I correct. "Who are you?"

"I'm Peter Brautigan, Ph.D. Remember?" Brautigan chuckles and shakes his head like I'm crazy.

"No. I mean. You know a lot about me. About my past. What about you?"

"Peter Brautigan, Ph.D." A patch of gravel sputters beneath us as we pass. "That's me. That's all you get."

We drive for close to two hours in silence before Brautigan says, "I was born and grew up very happily until I was thirteen and my mother and older sister died in a plane crash going to visit my grandmother. Afterwards I tried to take their place. That is, I tried to keep the house clean. And cook. I cooked. This infuriated my father. He said it was unmanly of me. But—at least I hope this is true—I think he just resented me trying to be them when they were dead, hated me for reminding him. I think he thought it would have been easier for him if I'd died with them. So he forbid me to use the kitchen. Or to clean any room but my own. And if I did clean my own, he wanted me to do it while he was at work. He didn't want to hear a vacuum cleaner or a trash can being emptied or the hiss of a dust rag on the shelf of a bookcase. The house grew so dusty it became hazy when you moved through it, rousing a trail of motes behind you. We started eating out every meal. Together, at first, then apart. Occasionally we'd run into each other coming into or leaving the same diner. Even on the occasions when we were both going into the same place simultaneously, we sat at different tables. I stayed out of the living room, where he watched television. I stayed out of the laundry room, doing my clothes at a neighbor's house, who somehow, without ever asking, understood exactly what was going on. I started studying at school until the janitors made me leave. I took out twice as many library books as I was supposed to and, when I was home, hid in my room without stereo or radio to entertain my ears that ached at the stillness of our house. I read, which, when my father discovered that I was using my dead sister's library card to take out more books than I was supposed to, led my father to call me every name in the book. Sissy. Ghoul. Grave-robber. Girly. That sort of thing. Then I went to college on scholarship, met a girl who was wealthy through no fault of her own, married her, lived on her trust fund while in the throes of grad school, further in-furiating my father. Not being the breadwinner, I deserved nothing but his scorn. He died five years ago and left everything to the Humane Society, if you can believe it. I enjoy my job very much. I love my wife as much as I did when I first met her, but understand her less, some-how. My kids are very bright and not afraid to hug me in front of their friends, but they don't have much to say to me over dinner. I've pub-lished two not very exciting books about sheep-farming lore and the history of license plates. Lately, I've become obsessed with hiding in bushes and imagining myself leaping out to terrorize young adults. My student evaluations are usually mediocre to good." Brautigan paused and looked over at me for such a long time I felt the need to look away out my window. When I knew he had turned his attention back to the road in front of us, I faced forward again. "That's my story," Brautigan said. "That's who I am. It's a little pathetic, isn't it? As narrative, it's hopelessly maudlin. Wouldn't make a good movie or book or anything. Nothing exciting in it. Nothing legendary. I didn't have a great rec-onciliation with my father before he died. I didn't spend exorbitant amounts of money on his tombstone. I don't visit his grave or the grave of my mother or sister on special days. Except, and this should tell you how much the study of folklore has warped me, on el Dia de los Muertos I always buy one of those tiny sugar skulls they sell outside the languages department, and I take it back to my office and sit in the dark and eat it and remember a Halloween when I was very little and my sister went as Little Bo Peep and dressed me as a sheep. She covered my white pajamas with cotton balls and painted my nose black and put a little leash on me and I crawled around the living room going 'Baa! Baa!' I remember my parents laughing until they cried. That's how I remember them. That's how I remember all of them, on that night. Looking up at them from the floor and seeing them laughing. They all seemed very tall, and even as the sidewalks outside swarmed with ghouls and witches, I felt perfectly safe and secure."

We pass a sign that says, EL PASO 15.

"That's it. The end. Now you know my life story. Feel better?" Brautigan sounds a little sad, a little bitter.

"I don't know," I tell him. "Do you?"

"I don't know." He shakes his head, genuinely puzzled. "I just don't know."

El Paso, I'm sorry to report, is one of the world's ugliest cities. When we come over a hill and see it stretched out before us like a riverside landfill shrouded in turd-brown smog, I feel like the reluctant hero of a sword-and-sorcery epic laying eyes on the lair of the dragon he must vanquish with nought to aid him but a toothpick. "It's hideous," I say to Brautigan.

He sighs. "Wait till you see it up close."

We drive into downtown as the office-building traffic is leaving. It's as if we are headed into the heart of a disaster that everyone else has the good sense to flee. The further we venture into the shadowy canyons, the fewer people we encounter in cars or on the street. Some of the signs, the bright billboards mounted on walls, are in Spanish, some in English, some in both like a textbook lesson.

"Did you ever see that Charlton Heston picture, *The Omega Man*?"

Brautigan nods. "I saw it in the theaters when it came out, and it scared the shit out of me."

"This reminds me a little of that," I say. "The empty streets and all."

Brautigan stops at a yellow light and guns the engine. "I saw it again, not too long ago, actually. It really sucked this time. Typical sixties movie. Too groovy for its own good. A lot of bad clothes, bad hair, hippie mumbo-jumbo. Hollywood just never caught on to hip."

We pull up in front of a building that I know to be the jail even before I read the sign declaring it so. It is neat, stark, yellowish bricks devoid of the graffiti that mar its neighbors' walls. "Here we are," Brautigan announces.

"Are we going right in?"

"Why? What? Did you have somewhere else to be?"

"Well, I sort of hoped to freshen up a bit."

"To talk with a possible murderer?"

"Well, I don't know. It just seems that maybe we should find a place to stay before we take this on. Maybe we should call first. You hate to just drop in."

"I called this morning before we left," Brautigan informs me. "The sheriff said we could come by whenever, stay as long as we like, sit in on any interrogations. Jesus, we're not coming for dinner."

"And that's a good point. Maybe he's eating dinner. I'm hungry myself." I rub my belly with my hook.

"So what you're suggesting is, we should go check into a motel, grab some chow and then come back? By then he'll probably be asleep."

"So we could come back in the morning. When he's better rested. You know how when I'm tired I don't feel much like talking and we get absolutely nothing done."

Brautigan, hands resting on top of the steering wheel like it's the back of a pew in church, sighs. "OK. We'll come back in the morning."

We check into a hotel, Eden, which promises FREE breakfast, FREE HBO, FREE local phone calls, FREE airport shuttle, FREE Juarez tourist information and FREE cocktails at happy hour. From the outside, it looked like a plain, uncomplicated, though somewhat gigantic inn. Once past the check-in, however, things become surreal. The Atrium, a word capitalized by the signs directing us to it and the desk clerk's rolling Latin tongue, towers and sprawls like a massive terrarium, replete with slender palms, innumerable ferns, an absurdly white gazebo floating on a pond lush with koi and gurgling waterfalls. Somewhere, a piano player, buried perhaps beneath a canopy of ivy and orchids, serenades the paradise with a high-pitched rendition of "Embraceable You."

Brautigan and I stand like caravan castaways stumbling upon a mirage so fantastic we dare not move lest we upset its spell.

"Excuse me," a passing bellman announces, his cart heavy with our bags.

"Can we afford this?"

"The department's picking it up," Brautigan says. We don't look at each other, but stand a moment longer. I crane my neck to see the rainbow prisms that dangle one hundred feet or more above our heads, suspended from the glass roof like giant icicles.

Finally, Brautigan, shaking himself free from his revery, says, "Come on. We're on the seventh floor."

When Brautigan knocks the next morning, I'm already up and dressed. The tie feels strange around my neck. I haven't worn one in so long, it was difficult for my fingers to remember how a knot is tied. My hook was of little help; it threatened to snag the silk and tear a gaping hole in the polka-dot landscape.

"Free breakfast," Brautigan says when I open the door. "In the Atrium." Noticing my outfit, he does a double take. "Nice," he said. "I like the dots."

"I thought maybe I should try to look official."

"For who?"

I usher Brautigan out the door and shut it behind me. "For whoever. The police, I guess." The smell of bacon and eggs wafts up from the Atrium Café. While we wait for the elevator to come fetch us, I peek over the railing. A buffet near the gazebo overflows with fruits and pastries. I still can't see the piano player, but he or she is there all right, wiggling through "Flight of the Bumblebee."

Seconds before the elevator dings its arrival, Brautigan says, "You've got a tag showing," and moves to help me fix myself. "We don't want you looking like an official mannequin."

We drive in absolute silence, don't say a word getting out of the car in the jail's cavernous parking garage.

In the elevator, I can hear the cables whirring, pulling the car next to us up, lowering us deeper and deeper into the lair of what? Who? The police? The Axe Man? Never before and I'm sure never again will I crave the depravity of Muzak.

I hear his voice before I see him. Indeed he isn't, except for his voice, even in the room. His words echo between the cinder-block walls, flat, unmusical, sounding too much like a NASA voice counting down to liftoff. In the room we occupy, two men sit at a table eating breakfast burritos, listening to the voice. When Brautigan and I came in, they hardly looked up, but continued squeezing packets of hot sauce onto the rolled tortillas, the red picante brutalizing the pale yellow eggs. Occasionally, one of them pricks up his ears, listens a moment, then makes a quick notation on a yellow legal pad. The other one nods slowly while he chews. "I prefer a nice hatchet," the voice says. "Or a tomahawk. Like you can get at a five-and-dime. Except with a real blade. But painted Injun-style. Maybe a few feathers on the handle."

Finally, one of the men, the nodder, says, "You Brautigan?"

"Yes."

"Come have a look." The nodder jerks his head to the side, beck-oning us closer.

We move carefully, unsure of what it is we're supposed to look at. When we're both directly behind the man, looking over his shoulder, he motions his head backward. "That's him," he says. "He ain't shy."

"Where?" Brautigan asks.

"In the box. Through the window. He can't see us. You know, the old mirror trick. You're familiar with it from television, movies, I'm sure." The nodder jerks his head back again, lifts his half-eaten, well-sauced burrito up and, using it as a pointer, motions behind him.

When we turn, the disembodied voice suddenly finds its master. There he is. Sitting, slouching really, in a sturdy wooden chair in a tiny bright room. A man in a gray suit sits across from him, smoking a cigarette.

"That's him?" I ask.

"Not the one smoking. That's Detective Mesa. The other one. That's him."

I expected more. From myself, that is. I expected some sort of psychic-link feeling, a shortness of breath, a dizzy sensation, maybe just the hairs on the back of my neck tingling. But looking at him, I feel nothing special. I may as well have been watching a talk show on television. Even the officers in the room with me seem bored silly. There is no sense of raw, infinite evil emanating from the man, filling the room and dimming the electric lights. Nobody sports a lei of garlic or, that I can see, a thrice-blessed crucifix.

"Slote Mashburn," the note-taking detective says.

"What?" Brautigan's voice, for some reason, is lower in pitch suddenly, sounding very manly and rough.

"His name. Slote Mashburn. Male Caucasian. Age: forty-two. Height: five two. Weight: one forty-four. Occupation: unknown. Place of birth: Topeka, Kansas. Favorite color: blue. Takes his coffee with sugar and cream. Doesn't mind if we smoke, but has never touched a cig himself, 'not ever' he says. Graduated from high school. Two years of college. Would prefer that we call him Slote rather than Mashburn. Says we sound like cartoon characters otherwise. Speaks in complete sentences most of the time. Just to dig at us, I suppose. You can go in if you want."

Brautigan turns to me. "You want?"

"Yes," I say. "Why not?"

When we go in, we carry two chairs with us. I'd expected them to make Brautigan leave everything possibly dangerous outside the Box, but they don't even search his briefcase. As we enter, Detective Mesa stands and excuses himself. "Bathroom," he whispers.

I look at Brautigan, wondering if he feels as strange as I do about being left alone with Slote Mashburn, the alleged Axe Man, terror of America's mall shoppers. Brautigan doesn't return my gaze, but opens his briefcase and takes out his tape recorder.

"No, I don't mind it a bit, Professor."

"I'm sorry. What?" Brautigan says, trying to sound in control.

"I don't mind being recorded. But I must warn you, the tapes won't come out. Everything I say will be garbled, backwards-sounding. Sorry, Prof."

"I'm not sure I understand."

"What, how do I know who you are?" Slote shuts his eyes tightly. "Brautigan. Doctor. Peter. Of Alpine, Texas. Lecturer in folklore. Sul Ross State University." He opens his eyes again and smiles, showing a mouth full of teeth that are somehow too small for his face, giving him a rodentine appearance. "My detective imitation." He looks past us and waves at the mirror on the wall. "Hello, boys."

"You're psychic?"

"No, Swifty. They told me you were coming."

"So, that, what you said about the tapes being worthless, that was a farce, as well?"

"What do you think? That I'm evil? The devil incarnate? Are you a researcher, my friend, or an exorcist?" Slote leans back in his chair and stares at the ceiling. "For I am the Alpha and the Omega, man." He quickly looks down and finds my eyes. I heard what he said, recognized the *Omega Man* reference, but keep a straight face. "Tapes. Tapes. Tapes. Why don't you just rewind to see if you can hear me? Or hear if you can see me."

Brautigan stares at him.

"Do it," Slote says. "It'll drive you crazy otherwise, wondering."

Brautigan leans to the recorder and rewinds.

Slote keeps his eyes glued to my own. He's very thin, gangly, balding a bit on top. He has perfect skin, however, skin that appears never to have been in need of a shave, little boy skin. His cheeks are rosy, like an ice skater just coming in from the cold. I can see how, if you were to put a wig on him and a dress, he might easily pass for a woman.

Brautigan presses play.

"For I am the Alpha and the Omega, man," the tape recorder bleats tinnily.

"You," Slote says to me, "were not mentioned by the boys in blue."

"My assistant," Brautigan says.

"Yes," Slote says, slowly, as if he is speaking to a child or inferior. "And does your assistant speak? I hope so. Sign language would be a mighty chore with just one hand and a hook. You'd have to move twice as fast to be heard."

"I'm Leonard," I say, proffering my good hand.

Slote doesn't move. "As a young boy," he says, "Leonard wandered the fields of the garden and never feared the snake that crawled there murmuring secrets and prophecies." Suddenly he lunges forward to grab my hand and pump it furiously. "You know why he brought you here, don't you?" Slote hisses at me. "You're Rikki-tikki-tavi, and I am a very nasty cobra." Still holding my hand in his own, he states calmly, "We're supposed to fight to the death, you and I." His voice becomes loud, raucous, ridiculously emphatic. "Announcing the world-champion bout of the century, a one-time-only confrontation to shock the nation: Hook Man versus Axe Man, live and in person. At last, two boogeymen, one event. Godzilla meets King Kong. Goliath meets Goliath. Winner takes all. Get ready to r-r-r-r-r-rumble!" Slote lowers his voice to a humming buzz, leans forward a bit. "How do you cure the man who thinks he's Jesus? Introduce him to the real messiah; that'll fix him or fuck him up but good."

I pull my hand away from his. "I don't know what you're talking about." I try to keep my voice steady, but know, somehow, that he felt my pulse race as he clutched my hand in his own.

"Denial, Doctor; that's what it looks like to me," Slote says, turning to Brautigan. "Of course, I'm not university-trained like yourself."

"So," Brautigan says, "you are the real Axe Man."

"Genuine. One hundred percent."

"Tell me," Brautigan requests, moving directly into what I now realize is his routine, "what is your earliest memory?"

"Excuse me," I say. "May I have a word alone with you, Dr. Brautigan?"

"Yes, of course. Will you excuse us?" Brautigan stands, nodding and bowing like a too-gracious host.

"Certainly. Your absence will give me time to decide upon a suitable earliest memory. I don't want to disappoint you with some lame story about fishing or goat-herding. This type of question requires an answer hinting at the spectacular or supernatural. A speck of Freud is often advisable in these situations, as well."

In the hall outside the Box I say to Brautigan, "Jesus. How did he know? About me being who I am."

"He doesn't," Brautigan says, smirking. "He's just playing with us. He saw your hook and decided to improvise a bit. He's really quite theatrical. Fascinating."

"I think there's something crazy going on here."

"Oh, yes. Sure. He may in fact be insane. There's always the possibility that he isn't really the Axe Man, but a knockoff of the Axe Man. A copycat Axe Man." Brautigan moves to open the door again. "Just try to act like you're humoring him. Go along with it. See what he says."

When we go back in, Brautigan eyes his briefcase. I do the same. Was there anything in there he may have snatched and squirreled away as a potential weapon?

"No need to worry," Slote says, allaying our fears. "Don't you think"—he waves a hand at the mirror—"the blue boys of Wonderland would have jumped all over me if I'd made a move for your briefcase?"

Slote rattles on for several hours about his exploits, none of which the police can confirm. Once or twice he mentions places and dates that would mean he and I were in the same location at the same time. Do I imagine that he looks at me when he mentions these shenanigans? Does he waggle his eyebrows, sneer in my direction, give me a psychic high sign?

The policemen, for their part, remain so calm they may be perched on the precipice of hibernation. Their slow, deliberate movements suggest a ballet choreographed to represent the dinosaurs in their final days, as the Ice Age overtook them and hung Popsicles off their scaly snouts.

But Brautigan and I are alert. I feel the sort of awakeness one is gripped by in the moments just after a car wreck, when every instant is like a Viewmaster slide, the colors too bright, the third dimension dancing like a chorus girl. Brautigan's tapes whirl and whirl. When one clicks off, finished, full, Slote stops and allows Brautigan to change sides or tapes before continuing.

"Listen," Slote says to me just after Detective Mesa slips Brautigan a note explaining he needs to wrap things up and come back tomorrow. "You believe me, right? You know what I'm talking about here."

I don't move, don't nod or blink or swallow to indicate any increment of agreement on my part.

"I know that you are who are, Popeye. I know where that dirty hook has rested, what car windows it's scratched at. I know the waiting game you play. We've got lots and lots in common, right? But let's get this straight, you and me, we're different beasts entirely. Different sides of the zoo. Different zookeepers bring us similar meals, but we eat differently and digest differently and sleep in ways that in no way resemble one another. Got it? You can take this two ways: as insult or absolution. We both have a thing for cars, true. And skulking, yes. And there are certain sharp objects you and me both keep close at hand. But. You feed off of dread, big boy. The creeping fear that surfaces at slumber parties and the like. You fuel the campfire-red faces of boys and girls just beginning to sprout hair and wants down there. But you're impotent. In this sense: you are harmless. You are nothing. You are a phantom in the end. A specter. A shadow rising from the earth, wielding a what? A prosthetic? Bushwa and humbug. Poppycock. Most of what they say about you isn't even true. Insane asylum escapee? You can't outrun the hum of everyday boredom, much less a top-notch security system. Dehooked again and again by Quarterback Andy's swift Camaro? Hardly. Rotting teeth, bloodshot eyes, maniacal laugh? Not applicable. You're a victim, my friend, of a nation's over-active imagination. You've spread like a contagion, like a plague of bad dreams. People dread you. But they never face you. They don't

see you. You see, you don't match the perception. You can walk the
streets safely and stalk the night happily and and and and and.
Your work is done. You're in. The big club of legends. We've given up
on Paul Bunyan and Johnny Appleseed. They don't work. Do-gooders
don't do it for anybody anymore, don't cut the mustard, make the
grade. We want villains. We couldn't give a flying fuck about Disney's
white-taffeta heroines, dickless Prince Whosits. But those bad guys?
Delicious in black! Evil-filled truffles: buy them by the dozen, gulp
down two at a time. Milquetoast-Duds? Pointless. Tasteless. Hopeless.
Chocolate-covered Scaries? Yum-yum. Ah, yes. You made your mark
with dread. But how long does dread last? Forever? Hardly. Dread dies,
too. Dread is mortal and mortally wounded by time, and time moves
now like the Concorde. We used to have dreads that lasted centuries.
Death. Hell. All that rot. Now they come and go. Polio. From dreadful
to dreadless to extinct in no time. Out with a whimper. Cancer? We
used to dread it like there was no tomorrow in its cellular wake. Now
it's everyday. Even movie stars can get it, and we don't care as much
as we might about what chemo horrors call Betty Boop to come on
down to the lab for another hair-stealing adventure. New diseases
come along, yes, bringing with them their dread-lined luggage, brimming with symptoms and benefit concerts. But scientists, those flaky
saints, treat dread like a puzzle and, after much chin scratching and
wallet snatching, solve for X, Y, Z and VD. Dread is dead, amigo. Your
reign, even as it is made more gruesome with gooey details and
budget-bulging special effects, nears an end.

"So, what's up next?

"The networks have canceled dread's prime-time slot and brought in some fresh young talent. Terror. That's my line. That's my slop. On the small scale, of course. I do it one to one, one on one, one foot in front of the other, one day at a time. Sweet Jesus, those pheromone explosions reek sweetly. Old bag shops hard, comes out to her lemon-fresh Caddy, thinking of an easy recipe to whip up quick for Dad and the lads and lassies, simple but tasty so they'll think she loves them more than to spend all day at the mall twirling sale racks like hula hoops. 'Dearie,' I say when they get in. Boo! Explosion one. Shock. Heart-racing, breathtaking. 'My daughter left me here by mistake,' or 'I'm lost. Could you give me a ride?' I say. But before they can put the old gas guzzler in gear, before their little pitter-patting corazóns have slowed back down to a nice leisurely stroll, I'm up off my axe and shaking it like a tambourine, like the instrument it is. Listen: You don't hear the tinkle of coins, a gypsy cacophony, some Partridge-girl hip-shimmy. But the screams? Just as lyrical. Tiny little voices they have at teatime, these darling suburbanites. In the cocoon of doom I've spun, they bellow like cows gone too long without a salt lick, screech like the Emergency Broadcast System. Terror, thick, like ketchup—a good brand, not generic—soaks me. And I get a hard-on. In my little old lady suit lurks the dick of an elephant. I'd show you, but you might find me perverse. Now, here's the question. What do I do with them? Do I swing hard and fast and leave Mr. Rent-a-Pig a nice surprise for his midnight rounds? Or do I let them leap from the car, and make a swift getaway to my motel room? Do I stay in a motel? Do I sleep in my car? Is it a van? Is there a sunset painted on the van's sliding door? A seascape? A desert? Or do I go home? Do I live with my mother still? My grandmother? Are those her clothes I'm sporting? Maybe I'm married. Maybe I have a wife and children. Maybe I'm a CPA. Maybe I live all alone. Maybe I have a collection of cigarette lighters from all the cars I've sat in. Maybe I take them out and roll around on them until I have an orgasm. And then maybe I'm okay and don't feel the need to taste terror again for a month. Or a year. Or a week. Or never. Maybe I've only done this once. Maybe I'm a copycat criminal. Maybe I read about the real Axe Man in the paper one day late, sitting at a bus stop. Maybe I've got an overactive imagination. Maybe I'm the only one left with an overactive imagination. Maybe I'm the only one left with an imagination, period.

"Terror. It lives in the heart and head and adrenal glands and that marvelous sphincter muscle.

"Dread? Dead. Movie monsters like Dracula? Nailed shut beneath a filmography that includes *Plan 9 from Outer Space, Bride of the Monster, Dark Shadows*. The new breed? Terrorists. Hit a building with a bomb, an airplane, a subway, a tourist-packed cellar at the Tower of London. We nuevo monsters need more than what you settle for, Hook. We need screams plus. We need to reach out and touch the victim, be she Ma Bell or Mabel from Cleveland. The only glass we like to scratch on is the TV screen during the five o'clock news. We need the scream pure, without filters, better yet amplified by the best RCA money can buy. Pump up the volume, etc., etc. You find your thrill in a blueberry patch, goosing the sexual anxieties of little Mary Jo and Billy Bud as they chug toward the end of what little innocence they retain. They're safe in their Chevy-sphere, like a snowman hunkered down next to Heidi's house in a snow globe. Let me *in* the snow globe. Let me grab that snowman's carrot nose and chase Heidi 'round

Grandpa's bed. Let me set the snowman's coal eyes and teeth and button on fire. Let me turn that snow globe into hell. Then I'll be happy. I won't sit on the outskirts of Shitville *imagining* the grief I can bring. I'll drive in and make myself at home, read the inside of your glove compartment while I screw up the electronic positioning of the driver's seat, the passenger's seat, the rearview mirror. Gremlin shit. Maddening, but not lethal.

"Your newsworthiness is without value these late-century days. You may, like Bigfoot, our grand legendary grandpa, find five minutes on some silly variety show, sandwiched between an Aztec ceremonial knife and an infant mathematician. You oddities! Museum pieces!

"But terror? Terrorism? Front-page stuff! Special logos on CNN! For us they will interrupt sitcoms, soap operas, *Star Trek*!

"Retire, old man. You've had your day, your scary, starry nights. Your frame in legend's Hall of Fame awaits. Throw in the towel. Hang up your hook.

"Hand the reins over to me."

Slote paused for the first time in this rant. "Aw. But listen at how I do go on. Lord help me, I'm a rambling man. Shall we call it a day?"

We return to Eden. Happy hour is commencing, and over the sound of the trickling waterfall, quacking ducks and tinkling piano ("A pretty Girl Is Like a Melody"), the blither of men and women ordering FREE cocktails and lying about their individual successes in life flourishes. "Shall we join them?" Brautigan asks, sweeping his arm in a grand gesture, like we are playboy millionaires perhaps, strolling into the casino at Monte Carlo, ripe to dazzle heiresses with our witty repartee and impossible luck at baccarat. I think of Duncan, standing somewhere behind a felt crescent even now, hands full of cards, bantering with a conventioneer who has just doubled down on eleven in hopes of replenishing his stake.

"I need," I say, "to freshen up first." The tie around my throat, no matter how much I loosen it, has begun to feel like a noose.

When I visited my brother once, his little girl—precious, tiny, red-haired miracle of honesty—clung to my neck like a monkey hiding from tigers in a tree. I shifted her from arm to arm while we stood outside, her father flipping steaks on the grill. "I saw a show on TV," she whispered in my ear.

"Really?" I asked.

"If you dipped your hook in a big bowl of frozen liquid nitrogen, it would be real easy to break. Like a china plate."

"Is that right?"

"On television the man did it with a banana and a hammer. He shattered the banana with the hammer. Then he frozed the hammer and shattered it."

"Do you like science?"

"Uh," my niece said. "If I were you, I'd be really sure not to get my hook around any frozen liquid nitrogen."

"I'll be on the lookout," I gasped, her arms choking the breath from me. "I'll be extra careful."

*   *   *

The red light at the top of my phone's dial pad blinks like a heartbeat. In the stillness of my room, it commands my attention immediately, as if a siren. While I pull the tie from my neck (sweet relief), I pick up the phone receiver with my hook and cradle it between my shoulder and ear. "Is there a message for me?" I ask the desk clerk when she picks up.

"Yes. It's on your voice mail. One moment and I'll connect you."

I wait, listening to the strange electronic silence, until there is a sudden high-pitched beep.

Music. Guitars. "Remember me to one who lives there," a familiar voice croons. "She once was a true love of mine." It's Paul Simon and Art Garfunkel. Calling me? No, it's a recording. The song continues. I listen, fighting the urge to hum along, until the song is over and the same high-pitched beep signals the end of transmission.

I hang up the phone and think a minute. Is this a joke, a new kind of phone prank; has the old Prince Albert in a can bit been retired and replaced by song lyrics?

"Yes?" the desk clerk says. "Can I help you?"

"Um, yes. I just called and got my voice mail. How do I go about hearing that message again?"

"I'll call it back up for you," she says. "Then, if you need to hear it again, just press three and the star sign. Hang on a moment."

After the beep—the roadrunner's clipped swan song—"Scarborough Fair" starts up again. Toward the end, I think, despite the poor sound quality, a third voice joins the duo's close harmonies.

Pushing three and the star sign as directed, I listen once again. There's definitely something there. A voice that is slightly familiar, a tad clearer than the song recording, someone adding his own tongue to the tune. "Parsley Sage Rosemary and Time," Simon and Garfunkel drawl like Gregorians. The third voice, though, seems to be saying something quite different.

After pushing three and the star sign several times more, I begin to imagine that I can tell exactly what the third voice is saying. It separates from the other two, stands out, speaks directly, clearly.

"Hurry Gage Rosemary There's Time."

Beep.

"Leonard," Brautigan says to me when I come into the bar feeling a little woozy, a little shaken by the phone message, "I want you to meet Isadora Lechuza." He indicates a woman sitting to his left, young, Hispanic, eyes bright and large behind a pair of thick glasses. "An old friend of mine."

Isadora stands and extends her hand. "Mr. Gage," she says. "Very nice to meet you."

When her fingers are about to meet mine, a spark of electricity jumps between us. "I'm sorry," I say. "I guess the carpet . . ."

"No," she says, taking my hand in her own and pressing lightly. "It's me, I'm afraid. It happens all the time."

"Isadora is a curandera," Brautigan tells me. "She's spoken to several of my classes."

"I live in Presidio," Isadora explains, taking her seat again. "But I wish I lived in Alpine. I have some relatives there."

"It's a lovely town," I say. "A curandera. That's a sort of healer, isn't it?"

"You win a prize. Most people don't know anything about it, and those who do don't know much at all. Usually, people think it's a sort of witch doctor. A Mexican witch doctor. People who come to see me for the first time, gringos at least, expect to find a house full of shrunken heads and pincushioned Barbies."

"What a pleasant surprise to see you," Brautigan says. He reaches across to pat her on the back of her hand. In the shadow made by his hand I see a spark, blue, twinkle at his touch. Brautigan's flinch is infinitesimal. "Oh, Leonard. Let me get you a drink. What would you have?"

"Just a beer," I answer. "Shiner, if they have it."

"Be right back," Brautigan assures us.

"So you live in Presidio," I say. "Are you here to visit relatives?"

"No," Isadora says. When she blinks, it's very slowly. I find myself watching her eyes, waiting for her lids to drowse and bow and close and rise again. "I'm giving a talk at UTEP tomorrow. On herbs."

"Oh," I say, trying to sound interested, but knowing nothing on the subject. I might mention that I subscribe to no gardening magazines and usually skim those articles in *Southern Living* that deal with planting magnolias or harvesting gardenias.

"Do you lecture much?" Isadora says.

"No," I admit, with a laugh, "I'm not a professor. I'm a—"

"I know who you are," Isadora cuts me off.

I watch her eyes grow even wider behind her lenses and find myself nodding, remembering about the spark that leapt between us.

"No," she says, smiling. "I mean, Peter told me about you. I hope you don't mind."

I'm surprised to find that I don't mind at all, that, in fact, I feel relieved that I don't have to act the part of academic. That I don't have the secret identity of a superhero, or supervillain or super-anything to hide.

"I have heard so much about you," Isadora says. "For so long."

"Really," I say. "I guess I'm flattered."

"Growing up in Mexico, you were mentioned every now and then, but when I came to the States, for college, you were the talk of the campus. It was said you struck there yearly. On campus. On the anniversary of the day you killed your wife. Soon after Valentine's Day, as I recall."

"Oh," I say. "Well, I've never been married, actually."

"Right," Isadora says, lifting her drink to take a dainty sip. "Where would you wear the ring, after all?" She waits to make sure that I'm not offended before laughing at her own joke.

"Well," Brautigan drawls, rejoining us, "I see you guys have found some way to amuse yourselves." He sets my beer down in front of me.

"Peter," Isadora says, "why don't you have Leonard talk to your classes, at least your graduate seminars? They'd love him."

Brautigan balks. "Well, I don't see how. I mean, I don't think Leonard would much care to."

"Would you?" Isadora asks me.

"I don't know," I say, looking at Brautigan to see if he might direct me toward the right answer. Then my desire to be in his classroom comes back to me, the need to be surrounded if only momentarily by the students. I nod. "Yes. I would love to speak."

Isadora laughs. "So. There you go. Peter, you must have him. And every guest lecturer you have is simply one less day for which you are responsible. You know," she whispers, leaning across the table toward me, her necklace, a tiny black stone on a cord of rawhide, swinging forward to ping against her glass, "you're all they want to talk about. The students. I've never been in a class where you didn't come up. What you mean. Where you came from. Why you do it. They love you. You're the rock star of folklore, I would say. Topping the charts for much longer than any Beatles ballad that I can think of."

"I guess I'm flattered," I say, trying to shut out the sound of the piano, still hidden, tinkling like mad. My mind supplies the words to its melody: parsley, sage, rosemary and thyme; Hurry, Gage, Rosemary, there's time.

"We could," Rosemary said, "have a perfect child."

We'd spiked a smallish watermelon in celebration of an all-night horror-movie festival at the drive-in. After only a slice, I felt a little out of control. "Huh?" I said.

"They're not genetic," Rosemary explained. "Our misfortunes. We're not destined to have children missing digits. We might—we would!—have beautiful children."

"Destiny!?" I thundered. "You and me, the Hook Man and the Kentucky Fried Rat Lady, we're not destined to bear a new generation of monsters?"

"Monsters?" Rosemary shrieked, spitting seeds. One landed on my cheek and stuck there. I flicked it off with the point of my hook. "We're monsters?"

I stumbled. "Well. No. But."

Rosemary propelled herself upward off the porch glider, spilling watermelon rinds on the floor around her ruined feet. "No buts about it."

"No hands," I said, knowing I should shut up, but unable to, my tongue so addled by rum it may as well have been the tongue of someone else. "No hands. No feet, maybe, but a butt he would have. He'd have a fine butt, our son!"

"Our son!" Rosemary sputtered, turning from the screen door to glare at me. "Our daughter, you mean."

"Our son!" I shouted. "Our son! No doubt decapitated at some point in his young adulthood, left to wander a pumpkin patch, searching for his beautiful head, fumbling about with hands his father worships, scrambling in the dirt and pulpy tendrils, desperate to find his gorgeous noggin. Fated to haunt a rumor-laden lovers' lane forever, alone, unloved, feared." I stopped, fought back the stinging tears. "They fear him! Our son! Our beautiful boy!"

Rosemary said not a word more, just shook her head and went inside, leaving behind a half-eaten watermelon, a swarm of flies feasting on its sugary pink innards, and me.

*   *   *

When Brautigan excuses himself to go to the bathroom, Isadora scoots her chair over close to mine so that we're sitting side to side, like theatergoers. She leans close to my ear and, her voice deep and calm like a hypnotist's, says, "You're going to drive yourself crazy."

"What?" I say. I try to turn to face her, but she holds her hand cupped around my ear so that I would have to fight her to move at all.

"You're a mess. All this pain and worry and confusion. About—good God—everything. Let me come up to your room later. I can fix this."

"I don't know. What would Dr. Brautigan think?"

"He never has to know," Isadora says. She moves her hand away from my ear so that I am free to move again, but it takes me a second or two before I can bring myself to face her.

Later, after Brautigan and I have walked Isadora to her room—on a much lower floor—and said our own good nights, I sit on my bed, wondering if she was serious, if she would be coming to my room. Wouldn't it be easier if I just went to her room? As it was, Brautigan might still be awake when—if—she showed up at my door. He'd hear her. Then, too, what did that matter? They're clearly friends and nothing more.

I get up and look at myself in the mirror. A bead of sweat rolls out from under my arm down to my elbow. I think about changing shirts. About taking my clothes off completely and getting into bed, feigning sleep. About kicking off my shoes. About peeling off my socks. About going to the bathroom and brushing my teeth. About opening one of the magazines I brought and rubbing a perfume-ad strip across my wrists, behind my ears. I think about all of these things but do none of them. Instead, I back up and sit on the edge of my bed, dreading and hoping for the rap of Isadora's fist against my door.

When the phone rings, I jump. "Hello?"

"Remember me to one who lives there . . ."

"Hello? Hello?"

"She once was a true love of mine."

Click.

Isadora's knock, like a raven pecking at the brass plate on which my room number is engraved, wakes me. I sit upright and look at the phone. I don't remember putting the receiver on its cradle. I don't remember leaning back on my bed. I don't remember falling asleep. "Just a minute," I half say, half whisper at the door. "I'll be right there." I run a hand through my hair, hoping to calm it from its struggle against the pillows.

When I open the door—with the chain on it—and peek out, Isadora says, "Open up. It's me."

Looking down, I note that she's holding a burlap sack.

"Hang on," I say, closing the door and unchaining it.

"What were you doing?" Isadora says. She hasn't changed clothes or re-fixed her makeup, and my nose tells me that there is no change in the way she smells, no perfume was spritzed on for my benefit. She bustles past me.

"I fell asleep, I think."

"Jesus," she says, setting her bag down on the dresser. "You'd think you were expecting a boogeyman the way you had that door locked and chained." She turns to face me, knits her eyebrows. "Hey, this sort of reminds me of an old Abbott and Costello movie. Remember the one where they meet the Wolf Man?"

"I don't think I ever saw that particular film."

Isadora begins to take things out of her bag and arrange them on the dresser top. "It's a good one. And there's this scene where the Wolf Man, whatsisface, Larry Talbot. Wait." She stops and bites at a long red nail. "Is that the character's name or the actor's name?"

"Dunno."

She nods and shakes her hands in front of her like she's drying them off, then goes back to rummaging through the bag, pulling out several candles, then putting them right back in. "Doesn't matter. Anyway, he knows he's the Wolf Man, right? And there's a full moon, and he knows he's going to go, you know, lupine at any minute. So he tells Abbott and Costello to lock him in his motel room and not let him out no matter what they hear happening inside."

She pauses.

"Right," I say. "And?"

"And what? That reminded me of you holed up in here like you were. Sort of."

I don't know whether I should approach her or wait for her to finish and approach me. I try not to stare at her or the bed but at my feet. They don't look real. They look, for some reason, like they are someone else's feet, like they are not attached to my own body. I look away from them and focus my attention on a mosquito—hatched no doubt from the lobby's ridiculous lagoon—that has somehow gotten in the room. It fumbles around the dresser lampshade, tickling the lightbulb.

"What is all that?" I finally say, driven to speech by my discomfort.

"Tools," Isadora says. "We're almost ready to get started." She fishes a large hotplate out of the bag and plugs it into a wall outlet. Then, wetting her finger and feeling to make sure that the burner is getting hot, she reaches into the bag and pulls out a shallow cobalt-blue bowl, which she sets on top of the burner. "Be right back," she singsongs, waltzing into the bathroom. She doesn't close the door behind her.

Is she getting undressed? I wonder. Should I do the same?

"I'm back," Isadora sings immediately. The ice bucket sloshes in her arms. Pouring the water into the cobalt bowl, she says, "Okay. Now we sit down and talk." She dries her hands on her sleeves. "Give this a chance to steam up."

"You're looking at me funny," Isadora says.

"No. I'm just. Not sure how this works."

"Well, you've never done it before. You can't know."

Taken aback, insulted, I blurt, "Hardly. I'm experienced." Immediately I realize how much I sound like a boy defending himself against the truth of his inexperience. I look away from Isadora, cough into my fist.

Isadora cocks her head to one side so that her hair falls like a black wave over her left ear. She blinks her strange slow-motion blink, then squints at me. "I see. You think. You think something that is not quite right."

"I beg your pardon."

Isadora smiles at me, gets up from her chair and moves to kneel beside mine. She takes my hand in both of hers—two little sparks— and squeezes. "I don't want you to be embarrassed."

"I—"

"No," Isadora insists. "Just listen. This isn't about sex. Not between you and me, at least."

I try to pull my hand away from her, but once again she holds tight, so that I'm left no choice but to sit still.

"I'm sorry if that's what you thought. And it's not that you're un-attractive. You're quite handsome. But I had something else in mind. Something more important."

"Oh, God," I say. "I feel like a dope."

Still holding my hand, she stands. It's the first time I realize how tiny she is. The stone hanging from her neck is level with my eyes.

"Listen," Isadora says, "we've got work to do, and there's no room in this line of healing for shyness or discomfort." Letting go of my hand, she turns and moves back to her chair. "I'm going to show you something," Isadora says. She holds out her hands. I hadn't noticed her picking anything up off the dresser or taking something out of her pockets between the time she held my hands and now, but there is indeed something there, cupped in her joined palms. Dark, tiny, it begs me to lean forward for a closer inspection. "Do you know what this is?" she asks me.

I do, but am unable to speak. It's a fossilized sea urchin, the same kind Rosemary found in front of her house in Wichita Falls, the same kind I took to school so many years ago, when Mrs. Custer told me I'd found something quite common, something unremarkable.

"It's a heart," Isadora says, her voice a ghost voice, the echo of a rattlesnake's tail wag. "A heart."

"It's . . ."

"A heart," Isadora says yet again. "Fossilized. Millions of years old."

"Are you sure?" I ask.

"Take it," Isadora tells me, leaning forward. I hold out my palms just as I did in that hot fourth-grade classroom and Isadora tilts her hands so that the sea urchin/heart rolls forward, end over end, until it perches at the edge of Isadora's fingertips like a miracle of nature, a hanging rock, a boulder balanced on the lip of a desert canyon. Then, gravity taking hold, it tumbles into my grasp, carrying with it a spark from Isadora. "Hold it tight," she says. "Hold it tight like it's your own heart, like its presence in your hand is all that's keeping you alive."

I do as Isadora instructs me to. My hands wrap around the sea urchin/heart like a child holding tight to a kiss thrown by a favorite aunt. I feel its ridges and markings on my palm, against the fleshy pad at the base of my fingers, the hard muscle at the bottom of my thumb.

"Do you feel it?" Isadora asks.

"Yes."

"No. Do you feel it? Its life? Its beat?"

I start to shake my head no, to tell her that what I hold in my hands is not a heart but a water thing turned into stone. I start to open my hands to drop the sea urchin on the sculpted shag carpet at my feet.

But.

But then I feel it. I do. Its beat. The thud of its life force.

"It's warm," I say.

"It will get warmer still," Isadora assures me. "It will get hot. But you can't let go. It won't burn you."

"I can feel it," I say, amazed.

"Yes," Isadora says. "I know."

"I can feel it beating like my own heart."

Isadora walks to the dresser and her bag. "Close your eyes." She looks at me. When she blinks, in slow motion, my eyelids follow her lead. But they don't open back up. They stay sealed shut.

"I can feel—"

"Shhh," Isadora says. "Shhhh."

When I feel the spark of Isadora's touch against my hands, I don't jump; I open my eyes. Some time has passed since I closed them, but I can't say how much.

"What do you feel now?" Isadora asks me.

"It's not quite so warm now. And I can barely feel it beating."

"Keep holding it," Isadora says. "Close your eyes again."

"Now what do you feel?"

Isadora kneels before me again.

"I feel," I say, and I am suddenly on the verge of tears, "nothing. It's gone."

"Give it to me," Isadora says. She presses on my hand so that it gives a little. My fist softens, and the stone falls into Isadora's right palm. With her left hand, she takes my fingers and pulls me up. "Come," she says.

Isadora holds the stone a few inches above the bowl on the burner. The water is boiling. Steam rises in wisps. "Relax," Isadora says.

I'm standing beside her, shaking a bit.

"Close your eyes," Isadora says.

In the darkness, a few flashes, like heat lightning. Then, a redness swells up to overtake the blackness. It's hard to breathe for a moment. Then the redness fades. Everything is black again.

"Open your eyes," Isadora says.

The stone is gone. Isadora dusts her hands the way a cook does after rolling dough. "Lean forward," Isadora tells me. "Breathe normally." She puts her hand in the middle of my shoulders and presses me down toward the steaming bowl.

The smoke recalls something I haven't smelled in some time. I can't put my finger on what it is.

"Should I close my eyes?" I ask Isadora.

"It doesn't matter," she answers.

Persimmons. I have to move a bit. Away from the tree. Its branches, like the bones of a bird's wings, a hundred birds' wings outstretched, are dotted here and there with persimmons. Not yet ripe. Bite down on one and your mouth will pucker and cry out for water. Persimmons. Sour little apples. They hang like tiny moons, obscuring my view. Where is it? Orion? Where are you?

Like a movie star, she moved through the halls followed by a retinue of servant peers. Glowing. Yesterday she moved through the light of a projector in science class. The Milky Way stretched across her smile. A nebula spiraled in her eye. Halley's Comet flamed against her lips. A meteor shower washed her hair before she sat, disappearing in the classroom's oblivion.

My brother had a box of Playboys *secreted in the barn. We looked at them cautiously, afraid every stomping horse's hoof was the boot of our father come to kick our asses. "She's beautiful," my brother said of every month's bunny. He shut his eyes to kiss Miss May.*

    When I shut mine, I saw Audra.

Homework for tomorrow: Find Orion.

She rarely rode the bus home. Most days her mother picked her up in their gleaming Jeep. Its very mud spatters looked perfect, perfectly placed, colored, textured. But when she did ride the bus, those after-

noons were cast always in golden light. No clouds could dampen the aura that surrounded her. She got off just before my brother and myself. After a second or two of readjustment, the school bus and its riders became itself and themselves again. There was nothing glowing or beautiful about any of us. Behind us, however, receding in our vision, diminishing, shrinking, she gathered the mail from her mailbox and moved like an angel to her front door.

I find the Big Dipper. And the Little Dipper. No problem there. Cassiopeia provides little resistance. Perseus. There he is. Just above and to the right of that highest persimmon. But Orion? AWOL, for all I can tell.

They'll give you the shits, them persimmons. Not ripe like they are. Don't go eating too many. Never mind too many. Don't go eating none. Wait a while. Keep your shirt on. All good things to the boy who don't cry wolf.

Leonard, she whispered in the library. I was looking for nothing but privacy. She surprised me; I expected her glow to precede her, announce her arrival like a herd of trumpeters calling heaven down to earth. Leonard, do you think I'm pretty?

*   *   *

She's pretty, my brother said. He kissed Miss July.

Look for the tip of his bow.

*The bus smelled like ammonia. Do you smell that? I asked my brother.
Some planets that's all there is. No oxygen. No water or nothing. Ammonia, that's all. And there may be life there anyway. Things that live
in ammonia.*

Smells terrible. Smells worse than persimmons.

*I stood in a corner next to the water fountain. The bell for Homeroom
ached to ring over my head. Buzz stood next to me, counting condoms
in the pocket of his jacket. When they passed me, Audra and her min-
ions, she sparkling like a firework, they basking in her glittering wake,
she turned to smile at me. I blistered to step out of the corner and join,
not them, but her, to have her take my arm and the two of us lead the
whole crowd off to a picnic, a football game, a Valentine's dance.*

Miss December tastes bad, my brother said.

*I was the oldest boy on the bus, the only male in my class not to get a
vehicle for some teenaged birthday. No hand-me-down farm trucks*

were available for my use. No ailing family wagon retired to the service of the kids was presented to me. No recently passed relatives bequeathed lemon-yellow Plymouths to this youth. I rode the bus like a well-respected spook. The younger kids, in deference to either my age or my prosthetic, avoided me, provided me with a moat of open seats to aid in the isolation I desired. When Audra rode the bus, she made it a point of sitting in front of me. I watched the halo above her head, the plumb line of her ponytail, like a fakir watches his snakes, with concentration so great it evokes headaches, begs for the admiration of tourists.

Just below that one. Is that a satellite? It moves so slowly. Too slowly to be a shooting star. When it comes out from behind that persimmon I'll know.

I heard it coming, the car, heard its slow approach, heard its engine growl as it climbed the hill.

Would you like to go out with me sometime, I said. My head hurt so much I thought I might pass out. My heart thudded in my chest like a jackhammer. I wished it might find a fault in the wall of my ribs and break out, ending my misery. We could go to a movie.

*   *   *

They're still green. You eat 'em while they're green like this, you're asking
for trouble. Asking for it.

What do you think about her? my brother asked me.
   Shhhh.
   What? Do you hear Daddy?
   No. I guess not.

Where'd it go? It never came out. I lost it. Was it a satellite? It moved
behind that persimmon, and that was that. That was that. Was it a
satellite or not?

The brightest star is in his belt. Note its coloration. What does that tell
us about this star?

Heard the growl of its engine over the growl of the oil wells, their arms
chugging, noses dipping, calling more oil to the surface, pulling it up
out of its home, charming it upward, day and night.

Oh, Leonard. You are sweet. You are. But I can't. I'm sorry. My mother
and father won't let me date yet. They're a little old-fashioned.

Maybe you could ask them. Maybe they'd say yes this time.

I could. Yes. I will. I'll do that. But I don't expect they'll say yes. Daddy's such an old sourpuss.

Heard the rustle of a footstep but didn't say anything this time. My brother held Miss October to his puckered lips. I closed my eyes and saw her moving down the hall, like a queen.

What are you boys doing? my mother asked.

Heard the engine's growl grow close. Saw the satellite move suddenly, unexpectedly from behind another much lower persimmon. It swept across the sky like the second hand of a clock, smooth, fluid. Heard the engine's growl.

Stars die sometimes. We can tell the age of a star by its color. What star in Orion do you suppose might die first?

Heard my brother gasp. But I didn't open my eyes. Heard my mother turn and leave.

It missed my head by not much. Its tires crept through the grass like a squad of rubber snakes, hissing against each blade, every cow patty, moving slow. Its headlights preceded it, searched the ground in front of it for rocks and trees too tired to stand up anymore. Its engine's growl became a murmur as it stopped and idled. The headlights slunk back to their caves, leaving all dark again.

Just one bite. Just to see what it's like. One bite. One time. Let's try it, my brother said.

You go first.

No, together, my brother insisted, handing me a fruit. Ready? On three.

Heard them giggling. Heard them crawling over the front seat into the back. Heard them breathing, like the rig pumps, deep, steady, pulling something up from its home.

You boys get your chores done? my father asked at dinner.

My mother stopped eating to look at me.

Yes, sir.

Yes, sir, my brother said.

I think mine's ripe. It's not that sour. It's sweet. It's like it should be.

Mine's terrible. Mine's like a lemon. Worse.

Mine's good.

*   *   *

Rolled over and crawled so slowly through the grass. Rocks scraped at my belly. My hand felt the edge of a hardened cow patty. Moved slowly. Careful. Don't make any sounds. Listen to see if they hear you.

Which star in this constellation do you think is the youngest? Why?

Heard them. Laughing again. Heard them. Say my name. Heard them. Laughing harder. Heard them.

We should burn them. We should get rid of them. We should take them to town and put them in the Dumpster behind the grocery store.
*   We could hide them someplace else.*

Pulled myself into a crouch beside the rear wheel. Heard my heart beating so hard in my chest I feared they'd hear it, too. Held my breath. Looked up. Saw another satellite moving into the arms of the persimmon tree.

*   *   *

Here. Drink this. I know; it tastes bad. But you'll feel better afterward. What did your daddy tell you about those things? Wait. Wait till they're ready.

Bright hubcap. In its reflection, the persimmon tree. The satellite. The tip of a bow. The point of my hook.

The bus stopped. Come on, my brother said, it's time to get off.

Heard them breathing. Heard them making sounds. So loud they couldn't hear me stand up, slowly, unfolding myself. Looking in through the rear window. Her face, eyes closed, her hair spilled behind her, falling off the seat, piling in the floorboard. His back, naked, muscled. His hands holding her hands above her head. Pinning her down. His two hands pressing hers against the seat. Her lips, moving. The glint of her teeth. Him pushing himself up off her. Her breasts, the nipples. Her opening her eyes, smiling up at Buzz. Her not seeing me. I'm there. Right there. But she doesn't see me.

I crouch again and move away. Into a maze of mesquite and cacti. Sit in a clearing, a circle of dust made by cows placing themselves in sleep. Miss December. Miss June. Miss March. Miss September. Look past the thorns at the car, still idling. The persimmon tree, peppered with sour fruit. Miss November. Miss April. The bright hubcap. Heard them. Saw them. Shut my eyes and see nothing now. Nothing at all. Hear them. The car idling. Smell the persimmon tree. Smell the satellites. Smell the oldest star in Orion, preparing itself for death.

PART | THREE

I see the first hitchhiker just before I cross into New Mexico. Highway 54 is lonely, stretching straight through the Fort Bliss Military Reservation. Much of south central New Mexico is NOT OPEN TO PUBLIC, the map I buy at a Chevron tells me. The gray screens used by the cartographer to designate these areas suggest a certain ghostliness, as if, were one to wander mistakenly into such a taboo landscape, one would find one's vision blurred with the passing of specters and phantoms. This is exactly what I think I see on the road in front of me, a ghost escaped from the military's zoo, a mirage, a trick of the eye and mind. She stands like a statue of Athena, arm and thumb outstretched. When I pass her, I slow just barely, not by hitting the brakes but by simply letting up slightly on the gas. She's pretty, young, not grizzled, not tanned leather-hard by the sun and a lifetime's experience on the road. She looks like a runaway, a girl grown tired of life under her mother's thumb, determined to escape the drudgery of homework, even after countless TV movies or school-assembly filmstrips detailing the horrors of hitching.

She looks vaguely like Heather from Alpine.

It's best not to get involved in these type things, I think to myself.

When I first got in the car, I could feel the outline of Brautigan's body underneath my legs. "It's not going to be easy driving a standard. Not with this." I waved my hook a bit, tapped it against the steering wheel.

"You're through with the easy ways," Isadora told me. She handed me the keys—pickpocketed from Brautigan in the bar last night—and shut my door, turned to go, sparks flying from beneath her heels. What will she tell Brautigan? I wondered, watching her walking back into the hotel's absurd lobby. When will she tell him? After he's been to the breakfast buffet for the second time? After he's heaped his plate with waffles and cream? Will he say, "I wonder where Leonard is?" Will she walk back inside now and go to his room? Will she wake him up and tell him I've stolen his car to get away from him and the Axe Man? Will she tell him what I've told her, what I've just remembered myself? Will she mention the petrified heart, its warmth and rhythm in my palm? Will Rosemary come up? Will Isadora make unexpected love to him before breaking the news of my getaway, affording me a few moments more before he considers his first step in the direction of my recapture?

Too many questions. I wiped them all out of my mind, all but one: putting the car in first gear, I asked myself, which way does one turn leaving Eden? Right or left?

*   *   *

Left.

El Paso fell behind me suddenly, suburbs thinning into a sea of heat waves washing over bare desert floor. The city and all its smells dissipated; the air grew clearer at every mile marker. In my rearview mirror, I could see, beyond my bloodshot eyes, a pall of smog squatting like a hen on a pile of rotten, shattered eggs. I was surprised to find that my hook feels remarkably at ease on the steering wheel. With the slightest pressure, I can move to pass cars, or swerve—ever so gracefully—past the occasional unlucky jackrabbit or turd-brown tumbleweed.

Once on the highway, car safely tripping along at sixty-five, I turned on the radio. There were no special songs on that I could find, no Willie Nelson anthems honoring travel or Boxcar Willie hobo serenades. I pushed the scan button and drove, smiling, listening to a three-second snippet of each station, one after another. For the most part, I caught the middles of commercials, ads for cars and Coca-Cola ("Muy Fresca!") and nightclubs proud to sponsor Wet T-Shirt Night, special appearances by male strippers imported from sunny, muscle-toned Los Angeles. I listened to the radio scan until the stations began to die out, one by one, until there seemed to be only two, battling for supremacy in the desert. Both featured accordion-heavy, Mexican tunes. I opted for the one that announced upcoming artists in Spanish *and* English.

And then I saw the hitchhiker.

*   *   *

Although she is so far behind me now I would be foolish to consider turning around in the middle of the highway and going back for her, I can't help but feel a little guilty. I wonder if she's cursing me for leaving her stranded like that. Of course, she's probably so used to the passing—and not-so-subtle slowing—of cars, I may not even be a memory. I may be so average as to be invisible.

I drive.

Judging by my map, I'm passing twenty miles or so to the east of White Sands National Monument when I see her again. The hitchhiker. She stands as before, on the road's gritty shoulder, patient, unassuming. Her hope dances on the tip of her thumb like a lone angel, cursing the philosophers who have driven away the rest of her heraldic crowd. I slow—same routine as before—sure that it will be a different girl, that her similarity to the nymphet I saw seventy-two miles ago is only just that, similarity. But even at the reduced speed of fifty, I can tell it is her. Once past her, I don't increase my speed, but slow even more, relishing her in my rearview mirror, simultaneously confused and somewhat spooked. When the heat waves engulf her, when her legs and breasts and head are so distorted by the sun's shimmer she might as well be a magician's assistant, boxed and rearranged by legerdemain, I turn back to the road in front of me. It's past lunchtime, but I am reluctant to stop, fearing that she will catch up to me with the aid of a more responsive motorist, afraid that she will come waltzing into whatever roadside diner may wait ahead, spear me with those eyes—clearly emerald even at high speeds—and leave me cold over a plate of onion rings.

I drive.

Once past Alamogordo, the hunger leaves me. I don't need to stop. I can careen further north, into the mountains my map promises.

I don't yet know where I'm headed. If I'm even headed anywhere. It would be possible to turn around right now, in the middle of the highway, and drive back to El Paso and Brautigan and Eden. I could lie and tell him I spent the day relaxing at a multiplex cinema or crossed the border to examine the wealth of piñatas Juarez offers its visitors. Still, my foot doesn't budge from its perch on the gas pedal. And my hook hesitates not a bit, but remains at the top of the steering wheel, like the maiden on a ship's prow, pointing, leaning, lusting for the unknown ahead.

I drive.

I drive into foothills of the aforementioned and much-anticipated mountains. The valleys are yellow sand dotted with scrubby mesquite, like the earth here is the hide of a jaundiced dalmation. I drive past innumerable rock shops as desolate as the one in Alpine. I drive through a tunnel as black as any night I ever stalked. I pass tiny oases of homes and trailers gathered around a stream that seems more trickle than water source, a dowser's good cry dribbling reluctantly downhill. I pass crosses placed roadside to commemorate the spot where someone, some unlucky James Dean, roared off into oblivion. Streamers hung from the arms of these crosses rustle only slightly as I pass. I cruise behind a convertible Cadillac driven by a man so short he might be a successful jockey; he turns off into a road that, for all I can see, goes nowhere. I motor behind a Volkswagen van with three "Eat Bertha's Mussels" bumper stickers and a license plate that reads 1 PEACE; when I pass they wave and smile and give me a thumbs-up; their stereo's vibrations push me ahead of them. I shadow railroad tracks that recall for me the chill of dead children pushing this car— this car I'm driving, the one I stole, Brautigan's car—to safety. I pass billboards advertising the availability of accommodations shaped like tepees, the impending opportunity—Don't Miss It, Pardner!—to visit Billy the Kid's cavernous hideout. I see mule deer running through fields recently plowed. Yellow road signs warn of falling rocks and the possibility that mountain goats may be crossing just ahead. I meet cars coming toward me with canoes strapped to their roofs, canoes every bit as bright as the one Rosemary and I paddled across a derrick-sprinkled lake some time ago. I face approaching highway patrolmen, merciless behind the armor of their mirrored sunglasses; my heart races every time I spy their cars and sharklike demeanor—do they know I'm on the lam? I pass stands advertising apples and apple cider, a gas station that proudly displays a flag from every state in the union and the chance to see a "real" rattlesnake nest or sample a rattlesnake taco while an attendant squeegees your windshield. I pass a tank around which are crowded a dozen or more cattle and a boy holding a cane pole in one hand, a can of beer in the other. I maneuver around curves echoing the yellow signs preceding them, over turtles day-tripping to the legendary other side, through cloud shadows that pound the convertible's roof with threats of rainfall. I drive.

I drive past the hitchhiker a third time. She's leaning against a sign indicating the peak immediately to her right is named Tularosa. This time, when I take my foot off the gas pedal, I remove it completely. The car slows.

In my rearview mirror, I see her walking toward me, her thumb still held out, but now close to her denimed hip.

It's not too late. I could still speed up, leaving her to rage at me in a cloud of xanthic dust. I could turn around and head back the other way, back to El Paso, back to the interrogation of the Axe Man, his interrogation of me.

But, instead, I take the car out of gear, lean over to unlock the passenger's door.

Third time. A charm.

Third time. You're out.

Third time. Impossible.

"I can't help but wonder," I say to her—Juanita Dark, she calls herself—after we're rolling again, "how you did it."

"Did what?" she says. She's lovely. Even her smelly feet, freed from hiking boots and resting lightly on the dashboard, are lovely, toenails painted a glossy pink.

"I passed you three times. I mean, this is the third time I've seen you. Did you get a ride from somebody who passed me?"

"I've never seen you before," she says, nonchalantly.

"Well, no. Of course not. I mean, it was easier for me to notice you than for you to notice me."

"Based on what?"

I don't know how to proceed, so I retrace and begin again. "It's just somewhat weird. I passed you just after leaving Texas, then an hour and a half later, and now, just now. How'd you do that?"

Juanita smiles. "You know."

"No. I don't."

She smiles harder, showing her teeth, perfect but for one incisor's exceptional length. A vampire? I wonder. Does she turn into a bat and fly the miles? In daylight? "Yes, you do," Juanita insists.

I laugh halfheartedly. "Really," I say, "I don't."

"So, where'd you get the hook?"

I blush a bit. "In an accident. When I was young."

Juanita nods. "Right. So. Get it?"

"No."

"Oh, come on," she says. "I know who you are. I knew when I got in the car. Surely you've got me figured out."

"I don't," I tell her.

She pauses. Out of the corner of my eye, I see her reach up to brush back her hair. "You don't?"

"I don't," I admit.

"So, are you the Hook Man, or what?"

"Who?" I lie.

Juanita frowns. "OK. I guess I was wrong. Sorry."

We ride for some time in silence. Finally I give in. "Yes," I tell her.

"Yes what?"

"Yes. I am the Hook Man."

Juanita holds a hand out to me. "Congratulations. On coming out." When I take her hand, I halfway expect a shock, like Isadora's. But it's a normal handshake. "I'm the Vanishing Hitchhiker," Juanita tells me.

I remember now. Brautigan's students, immediately before their discussion of myself and the Axe Man, spoke about the Bigfoot legend, and immediately before that about the Vanishing Hitchhiker. I was under the impression, however, that the Vanishing Hitchhiker was a ghost, not an actual person. I tell Juanita this.

"Right. Well, surely you know how these things get out of control, these legend-things." She pulls her feet off the dashboard and sets them on the edge of her seat, so her knees are pressed up against the fine down of her cheek. "The legend is—well, one of the legends is, there are, like, ten million variations—some guy passes me on the road a few times, and stops to pick me up. Sometimes it's close to a bridge or on a bridge and when I get in the car, I'm soaked. And I tell this guy where to take me in a ghostly voice, one of those you expect Mia Farrow to have based on how she looks. And when we get to the address, he gets out, this guy, and goes up to the door of the house, right? And my mother or father, one or the other, answers, and he says, 'Hey, I've got your daughter in my car, and she's wearing wet clothes, some kind of ball gown.' And my mother or father or maybe even both say, 'That's impossible. Our darling little girl was drowned ten years ago tonight. Her car went off the road, the bridge, the dam, whatever, and she was killed. She was on her way to the prom.' "

"Spooky," I say.

"You betcha. Sometimes they drive us to a graveyard. That's the address we sometimes give them, supposedly."

"Who's us?"

"Us. My sisters and I. That's the true part of the story, actually. Or the truth. Whatever."

I don't say anything. I don't look over at her picking the scab on her left knee, or adjusting the sunshade so she can see herself in its mirror. I drive.

"We're triplets," Juanita says. "See?"

"No."

"We're identical triplets." She pauses, apparently hoping that I'll jump on the truth with this added snatch of information. "Okay," she finally says, sighing. "We're identical trips, and this is our hobby. We race. From place to place. By thumb. Never together. It's like a scavenger hunt a little bit, or a grand prix. The Tour de France. It's like that."

"The Indianapolis 500," I try.

"No," Juanita corrects me. "That's a circle. We go places. We pick someplace on a map. Then we go. First one there gets to pick the next place."

"That sounds dangerous. Three girls hitchhiking."

"All races are dangerous. That's what makes them worthwhile."

"Okay," I say. "But I'm not sure I understand the whole Vanishing Hitchhiker story in light of the race motif."

"We're her. All three of us are her. Rolled into one. You thought you passed me three times. But you didn't. You passed Vivian, then you passed Delores. Or maybe you passed Delores, then Vivian. Then you picked me up."

"Oh," I say, the picture brightening so that I can recognize what's going on. "Very interesting."

"Yeah. It's a hoot."

I nod. "So you don't really disappear. And you don't really give anybody an address to your parents' house or a cemetery. You just hitch."

"Right," Juanita says. "I mean, I guess maybe it's possible that there really is a hitchhiking ghost somewhere, but it's not us. I figure people see us and make up the story to go with it. You have to admit, this conversation would be a lot more exotic if I were wearing a drenched prom dress."

"It's weird, isn't it?" Juanita says, smacking her gum.

"What?"

"How we grow. How our legends grow."

I think. "It doesn't really have much to do with us."

"No, it doesn't. We're like the spark that starts a fire. It gets out of control. You can't see the spark anymore for the flames."

"The forest for the trees."

"I guess," Juanita says. "But I wonder. About the second spark. Who is it that says more about us than there is to be truthfully said?"

"I don't know," I say.

"Are they paranoid? Really creative? What? To make something from nothing. It's sort of like magicians, kind of."

I think back to my experience at the Alpine post office, the bizarre Simon and Garfunkel phone call at Eden, the assumptions I made, the stories I might have concocted to explain the unlikely or impossible. "To make something from something else," I amend.

"They're more important than us, I think," Juanita says. "The second sparks. They notice us and make others notice us."

"Do we exist without them?"

"Does anyone exist without the acknowledgment of another?"

I think of Rosemary, how I've felt since she left, how my own existence without her has seemed less real. Still, I've had Brautigan at my side almost constantly, his interest in me incessant, unwavering. Is there a quality to acknowledgment that affects one's very being? "If a tree falls in a forest," I say.

"But what if there's a whole convention of lumberjacks there? They all hear it. Then they go home and tell their wives and kids about the sound.

"They'll each describe it differently.

"They may, some of them, embellish the story, say a giant pushed the tree down, that the sound they heard was the earth groaning at the impact.

"It could become mythical."

"Yes," I say, jumping in. "Civilizations might base their whole belief

system on one lumberjack's extravagant account of a toppled maple."
I remember my neighbor's home, each room bedecked in images of
itself, the wall space above the front door holding a picture of the well-
watered lawn, the asphalt street, my house, my shadow in the window.
Is that how my neighbor sees me, as a shadow? Did my quick tour of
her house affect her concept of me? Did the enormous drinks she
made affect that concept even further? When Juanita got in the car
she knew immediately who I was/am. Or at least she thought she did.
"You know me," I say to her.

"No," Juanita admits, offering me a stick of Juicy Fruit. "I know the
nine millionth spark. I see the flames of your imaginary past, feel them
flutter against my face like moths, but I don't know you from Adam."

When we cross over a cattle guard—set mysteriously in the middle of
the highway—the sudden vibration knocks something loose in the
backseat. It hits the floorboard with a thud. "What's that?" Juanita says,
waking up from light slumber.

"I don't know," I say.

Juanita turns around and looks down, then reaches back and,
grunting, hauls the log Rusty sent DeeDee up into the front seat with
us. She turns it like a player piano reading its musical scroll. "Cool,"
she says. "Paolo Pollo."

"What?"

"Did you make it?"

"No. It was sent to me."

"So somebody made it for you? That's really sweet. They must really love you."

"I don't know," I tell her.

"Oh, no. They do. This took hours."

"What," I ask, "was that you said? Paolo Pollo?"

"Right, yeah. Some of this is a Paolo Pollo poem. In Spanish. And some of it is I don't know what. Gibberish. Doggerel."

"What does it say?"

Juanita turns the log to what I assume is the beginning, although in all my examinations, I couldn't tell what was what, beginning, end, middle. " 'Tonight outside my window,' " Juanita reads.

Tonight outside my window bears stalk hummingbird nectar.
Starlight dusts their backs, snouts, delicate ears.

I hold my hand over my breast, trapping the heart that has
    squeezed through my rib cage, begs my nipple to set it free.

Bears sniff at my windowpanes,
leave love bites on the pine that guards my door.

My heart tells me it hears you calling my name,
tells me it can find you,
will bring you here to see the bears' signatures on my pine,
to let the starlight dust your shoulders,
to hear the hummingbird wings,
my heart, the river I've built to tell our story,
again and again down the mountain.

Be still, I tell my heart. Be quiet. Sleep.
All you hear, I tell my heart, are bears in starlight, stalking
     nectar.

"You speak Spanish?" I ask.

"A little." Juanita sighs. "But mainly I just know this poem. It's one of my favorites. Like I said, whoever sent this to you has got it bad."

"It may have been sent by mistake," I admit.

"I can't imagine that would be true," Juanita says. "Listen. There's more. After the poem, there's what sounds like Paolo Pollo, but it isn't part of the poem. I don't recognize it at all."

"What does it say?"

"It's in English, but the letters are like the stuff in Spanish, all run together. 'Come to noisy water and replace, sweet captain, the sun's cold arms with your own.' Any idea what that means? It's not Paolo Pollo."

I think about it for a moment or two. "No," I say. "I don't think so."

After another thirty minutes or so, I stop to get gas. Juanita leans against the car whistling while I pay. When I come out, she says, "You can leave me here if you're sick of my company."

"No," I say, walking around to the driver's side. With my door open, I lean across the roof and repeat myself. "No. Please. Let me take you where you're going."

"It's not much further," Juanita says, stepping back to open her door.

"It's not?"

She points to a road sign twenty yards ahead of us. "RUIDOSO," it says in reflective letters, "67."

"What prompted you to pick Ruidoso?"

"I didn't," Juanita tells me. "Delores did. *My* next choice is Missoula, Montana."

"That's a long haul."

"Yeah. Well. Ruidoso could be very nice actually. My guidebook promises lots of mountains and bears and a horse track and pine trees and streams. That's how it got its name. Ruidoso."

"How?"

"The streams. They run all through the town. And they're very loud. You know how little streams running over rocks and stuff make more noise than big, stupid rivers? They can be very musical."

"And that's why Ruidoso is Ruidoso?"

"That's what the guidebook says. Ruidoso means, in the Indian dialect, I guess, 'Noisy Water.' "

When she says it, she stops. I look over at her. Her mouth has dropped open. My heart is pounding. "Noisy water," she says again.

"Where's your guidebook?" I ask.

Juanita rummages around in her knapsack. "Here," she says, pulling out a dog-eared *Your Us & You*.

"Find Ruidoso," I tell her. "Read me everything."

*   *   *

There's a casino there, of course. Run by the Mescalero Indians on
their reservation. Doubtlessly the place Duncan had talked about going to. This must be it, the next stop on his blackjack tour of North
America. By the time I've told Juanita the whole story, all the details
of mine and Rosemary's relationship, we're pulling into Ruidoso, passing the first of the adobe tourist shops. We roar by the horse track,
empty but for a single horse and rider trotting leisurely across the
infield.

"Go straight to the casino," Juanita says. We've kept track of the
billboards touting the good fortune to be found at the Mescalero's Inn
of the Mountain Gods casino. "Find Duncan."

"Maybe I should stop somewhere," I suggest, "and get cleaned up.
I don't want to look road-weary."

"Screw that. Road-weary is precisely what you want. You want to
look like you've been driving maniacally for God knows how long,
searching endlessly for your true love."

I'm nervous, of course, almost sick with excitement and uncer-
tainty. "What if she doesn't want to see me?" I ask. "What if she refuses
to see me?"

"Listen," Juanita insists. "Anybody who wood-burns a Paolo Pollo
poem onto a log is hoping for some results. This," she raps her fist
against the evidence, "is no message in a bottle cast out on the ocean's
eternal facelessness. This was delivered by civil servantry's finest."

"But it wasn't really addressed to me," I remind her.

"Don't be such a stickler for details." She points out my window, her arm reaching under my chin. "Turn here," she commands.

The resort—that's what the Mescalero Inn of the Mountain Gods is, not just a casino but a full-fledged resort—is stunning. The buildings are dark wood, low, blending with the dense forests that press up against them. The lake, massive and blue, is dotted with fishermen casting lines into the mirrored surface. A golf course, its surreal green lawn fairy-tale perfect, stretches into the trees and disappears.

"There's the casino," Juanita says. "Pull up and park. I'll wait in the car."

"What if he's not here?"

"Then ask where he lives."

I hesitate turning the car off.

"You're wasting gas," Juanita says, reaching over to kill the ignition. "Go."

I look at her, imploring her to let me sit a moment or two longer.

She smiles. "I'll be here when you get back," she says. Leaning toward me, she kisses my cheek. "Go," she says again.

I've been in casinos before.

This one throws me for a loop. Instead of bright flashing lights, preening showgirls, hollering Texans at blackjack tables, there are only hundreds of slot machines. Where most casinos look packed to exploding with glitter and glitz, this casino is strangely empty. It's nothing more than a room, like a high school cafeteria. Indeed, instead of splashy neon Buddhas and Roman chariots, the decor resembles a halfhearted New Year's Eve party; tinsel garlands hang like vines here and there, strands of Christmas-tree lights snake from hook to hook in the ceiling tiles. Where most casinos are deafeningly loud, this one is no more cacophonous than a convenience store. A few women stand in a row at one wall of slots, each occupying two machines, plying them with quarters and yanking their bandit arms. In the center of the casino—the place is so sparsely furnished it can be taken in all at once—a cashier's cage is occupied by an obese Indian woman wearing a red vest; she pops bubblegum and flips the pages of a fashion magazine.

"Hi," I say, moving in front of the wire screen that separates her from the gamblers. Without looking up, she holds her hand out. Not knowing what she wants, I just stand until she moves her gaze from HOT PROM LOOKS to my face.

"What?" she says. "You want change?"

"No," I say. "Actually, I'm hoping to find someone who I think may work here."

She doesn't smile or nod, but stares.

"Maybe you know him. Duncan Swift? He's a blackjack dealer."

"We don't have blackjack," the cashier tells me. "Only slots. And video poker. Only machines. No wheels. No dice. No cards. Just the machines."

"Oh," I say, even though it's perfectly clear to me that the casino is bereft of such luxuries as wheels, dice or cards. "Well, I'm pretty sure he may have applied for a job here in the last year or so. Is there somebody, a manager or something, who I could speak with?"

"Yes," she says. Reaching down below the counter where her magazine rests, she pushes a button. "He'll be here in a minute," she says.

"Thanks."

"Can I help you?" the manager says, appearing suddenly behind me. He's an Indian, too.

"I don't know. I hope so." I begin to realize how silly this sounds, my questions. If Duncan came here, there was nothing for him to do, so he probably left immediately. "I'm looking for someone who may have applied for a job here about a year or so ago."

"Yes. Well," the manager says, "we don't take applications from outside the tribe."

"Oh, right. Of course."

"But I could check our files for you, if you'd like. We would keep a record of this person's interest. Why don't you come with me."

The manager's office is no bigger than a closet. We sit in chairs, knee to knee, while he talks. "Duncan Swift. I do remember him, actually. He wanted to deal for us. But we have nothing to deal."

"I noticed," I tell him.

"He had his sister with him. Wanted to get her a job, too."

"That was Rosemary."

"Yes. She dated one of our boys for a while."

I can't have heard him right. "What?"

"Duncan left. For Vegas, I think."

I suddenly feel very dizzy, foolish, ashamed to have worked myself into a frenzy of hope.

The manager continued, "And she, Rosemary, she got a job here in town. She works at the movie theater. Taking tickets. Selling them, too, I would imagine. I don't go to movies myself, but that's how she met Wes."

"Wes?"

"He's a Mescalero. I think she found a place to stay, in addition. A caretaker's cabin. She gets extra money in the winter, looking after a family's big cabin. A lot of people in town do that."

"Is she still dating him? Wes?"

"I don't know," the manager tells me. "You can ask him, though. He tends bar at the hotel. He's on duty now. Walk on over."

When I go out to the car, Juanita's gone. I should have guessed. Vanished. She's left a note, painted in nail polish, that reads, "Took the Paolo Pollo log—couldn't resist. Will you ever forgive me? Good luck and drive safely."

"Hello, Leonard," Wes says when I walk into the bar.

He's a miracle, as model-perfect as any young Adonis who ever stood glistening in a damnable cologne ad, and I'm even more afraid of him and his relationship with Rosemary than I was a few minutes ago. Tall, dark, handsome in the most Hollywood sense of the word, he wears the white shirt and bow tie of a bartender with real style, like

Tyrone Power or Cary Grant. He should be serving Nick and Nora Charles, not me.

"Hi." I stand in front of the bar, uncertain whether I should sit down or not. Holding my hook up, I wave it a bit. "The hook give it away?"

"The hook," Wes says, nodding. He sets a coaster in front of me. "Get you something?"

"Just a glass of water," I say.

"No problem." Wes picks up a tall Pilsner glass and fills it.

"You were expecting me?" I ask him.

"Months ago."

"What about Rosemary? Was she expecting me?"

Wes sets the water in front of me. "No," he says. "At least she told me she didn't."

I take a long drink. I haven't yet eaten any lunch, and it's way past dinnertime. Suddenly I'm starved. Reading my mind, Wes sets a bowl of pretzels in front of me. "Thanks."

"Listen," Wes says, leaning against the bar back. His white shirt, duplicated in the mirror behind him, swells and writhes with muscles. I look at myself in the same mirror and cringe. I look like shit, like a madman, wild-eyed, stubbled chin, hair a nest of greasy worms. I am as terrifying as any description an adrenaline-addled teen ever offered to french-fry-munching compadres. "Let's not be coy or manly about this. We're not seeing each other anymore. I'm far too young for her, she says, and she's probably right. Plus, she's still not over you. Frankly, I could not have stood another discussion of your bastardliness." He smiles. "You do sound like a bastard," he says. "But after every good cussing she ever gave you, I could tell she meant none of it, she'd take it all back if you were here, if it was you on her couch, not me."

I sigh, relieved. "Where is she?" I ask.

"My chivalry astounds me," he says, leaning away from the bar back. "I'll give you directions." He pulls a pen out of his apron pocket and writes on a coaster.

A tree grows through the front porch. Or, rather, the porch is built around the tree. It rises up through the wooden floor, up through the rafters and roof, rises higher still to tower over the dark, pine-needle-covered shingles. A hummingbird feeder hangs from the rain gutter, its ruby liquid calling a dozen or more of the minuscule birds to hover and buzz around the four feeder tubes. As I sit, summoning up the courage to walk up the stairs of the house whose address—written in perfect penmanship—I now hold in my good hand, one of the hummingbirds zips away from the feeder and alights on a telephone wire. I'm surprised, having been told at some time in my education that the poor birds never stop flying, that they live their entire lives airborne, fluttering. It sits only a moment or two; when another bird tries to join it on the wire, it flies away. The second bird, presumably an acquaintance of some kind, follows, like lightning chasing a kite.

"Here goes nothing," I say, and open the door of Brautigan's car.

Rosemary opens up before I have the opportunity to knock. "No," she says. "You're not coming in. Not yet."

She's beautiful. Tanned. Looking very strong in jeans and a khaki shirt with red epaulets. Her work uniform, probably.

"I," I say, "thought we might talk."

Shutting the door behind her, Rosemary nods. "We might."

But I can think of nothing to say. I spent hours driving up here, a long time listening to Juanita tell me what I should say to Rosemary, how to go about reassuring her that our love is nothing short of supernaturally predestined by gods. That kind of stuff. But I never thought about exactly what I wanted to say, how I could say it, how I could tell her what had been happening to me, what I'd been doing, what I'd been thinking.

"Okay," Rosemary says, filling the void I've created, "here's the deal. I've got to go to work." She walks to a moped I hadn't noticed before. "And when I get back, you can either be ready to talk, you can actually talk to me and say whatever it is you need to say, or you can be gone. Those are your choices."

I nod, like a student being given a homework assignment. "I can do that."

Rosemary gets on the moped and puts on the helmet that hung on its handlebars. When it's strapped on tightly, she says, "You can wait on the porch. Or in your car. But you're not going in my house. Not yet. Maybe not ever." She turns the ignition. Surprisingly, it makes very little noise. I'd expected a roar. "Be sure to look out for the bears, though." She revs the engine with the handlegrips.

"Bears?" I say, raising my voice a bit to be heard through her helmet.

"We're having a bear problem. They come after the trash. So when it gets dark, you might want to sit in your car. Or on the porch, you should be okay on the porch. Just don't screw with them if they come up. They'll take your head off."

She backs the moped away from me and turns it around to face the road. "It's good to see you," she says before she rolls forward, out of the driveway and into the road.

A minute or two after she's gone, I'm sitting on the porch when I hear the sound of the moped coming back.

"I've changed my mind," she says when she pulls up next to the porch.

I stand up, awaiting further orders, perfectly willing to do anything she asks.

"When I come back, you can either be long gone for good, or you can tell me you want to stay. I'm not going back with you. Wherever it is you came from. I like it here, and nothing's going to make me leave. You either disappear or you tell me 'Honey, I'm home' and mean it."

"I," I say.

"You think about it," Rosemary says. "You think about it and watch out for the bears."

I'm trying to decide what to do. But I can't get things to slow down long enough for me to look at them carefully. My thoughts, that is. Even though I know Rosemary won't be back for several hours, until the movie theater has closed probably, after all the couples have dragged themselves from the comfort and dark of the back row into the bright lobby and chill night air, I feel the need to rush. Did I come here to get Rosemary back? Did I come just to see her? Did I come to bring her back to Alpine? Did I know what I was doing when I let her leave with Duncan? She sat in his car, not speaking, while Duncan and I loaded the last of her things into the carrier on the car's roof. When I tried to get her to roll down the window to kiss me, at least to say good-bye, she sat very still, looking straight ahead. "Sorry," Duncan told me, opening his door to get in. "Sorry about all of this."

"It's not your fault," I said. I had a stack of magazines, some of my favorites, the ones I kept while on the road, the ones I didn't throw away but kept to thumb through again and again. "Here," I said, passing them over the top of the car to Duncan. "I thought you or she might like to read something while you drove. I don't know how far it is to where you're going."

"Well, I've got orders to tell you nothing more about that." He took the magazines and put them in the front seat, then leaned across to shake my hand. "I hope things work out for you."

"They will," I told him. "You take care of her."

"I'll try."

Then he got in and they drove away and I was left to pack my things, deposit the key under the doormat for the landlord, and hit the road, going east, going away, running for what I thought was my life.

*   *   *

It sounds a little like a calliope. I realize what it is almost immediately after I first take notice of its voice. A stream nearby is talking, singing, reminding Ruidoso why it is called what it is: noisy water. Looking around for bears even though there's still plenty of daylight, I walk down the porch steps, down the drive, and cross the road in the direction of the river's sound. Down a steep bank, through a thick screen of trees and brush, I catch a glimpse of blue-green motion. Carefully, using tree branches for support, I descend into the ravine, along what looks like a trail. It levels off and leads me to a clear area overlooking a bend in the water's path. It's wider than I'd imagined it would be, the river, and deeper-looking, too. I'd expected to see the bottom, the reason it gurgled so, expected to see the rocks, rounded and mossy and circled by trout. But a few feet away from the gravel shoals, the water deepens, turns dark and fast. There's a large rock nosing out of the river's middle, sliding up and out like a slate tabletop with legs cut too short on one end. From where I stand, someone—some Herculean engineer—has carefully placed assorted boulders in a line that jigs and jags from the gravel shore to the big rock; a brave or stupid soul might step cautiously from one to another to reach the large rock. Clearly there is enough room to sit on it, to stretch out even and, given the sun's cooperation, bask.

The temptation is too much to risk.

Step by step, stone by stone, I proceed, aware of the shifting my weight induces in every rock. The frightening sensation of having one's footing shiver in unexpected ways produces in me a state of euphoria not unlike that I've read (in God knows what magazine) occurs in temporarily lost spelunkers. When I reach the rock (the spelunker spots the lantern of a fellow adventurer or the bread crumbs Hansel left for Gretel's sense of security, or, yes sweet Lord, the light of day) I almost throw myself upon it, hug it. Instead, I stand for a second facing each direction. In front of me, downriver thirty or forty yards: a tiny, guardrail-less bridge just big enough for one car to traverse safely. To my right, the way I just came: the stepping-stones, the trail to the ravine's wall, Rosemary's house, invisible now behind so many pines. Behind me, upriver: more river, bending away into nothing, mountains peeking over sharp treetops. To my left: a wide stretch of deep water, then a gravel bank not unlike the one I left a few minutes ago. Pleased at my situation, my feat, at standing in the middle of the deep river, I can't help but feel good.

When I sit, the seat of my pants grows cold quickly. The rock is refrigerated by the water rushing around it. Testing the temperature with my finger, I'm surprised at just how close to ice the water is. Nevertheless, I can't help but take my shoes and socks off and dip, gingerly, each foot's toes in. Then I pull them out. When I stick them back in, this time a little further, the toes seem not to mind at all. Where they winced at first before, they seem now not to care, not to mind.

Again I remove and reinsert my feet, this time all the way to my ankles. Within moments, they've become totally numb. They are simply not there. They've been erased, like a cartoon character savaged by a gum eraser.

Over the sound of the river I hear a car approaching. It pulls onto the bridge and stops. The engine dies. Incredible: without hesitation, the boy driver leans over to kiss the female passenger. Passionately.

Without further ado, they abandon the discomfort of the front seat, the gear shift's threat and steering wheel's unyielding nosiness, for the roomy expanse of the backseat. Incredible.

Ignoring them (a feat, I must admit), I lean down and roll up the legs of my trousers, the ones I bought to be more like Brautigan, to be more real, more professional, more a part of the normal, daylight world. Then I stick my feet back in, this time to midway up my calves.

It is not long before my lower legs are virtually nonexistent.

So this is what it's like to be without feet.

So this is what it's like to be without legs.

So this is what it's like to be without knees.

I lie back against the rock. It would be no problem to simply slide down into the water, a little at a time, until there is nothing left but my head, bobbing disembodied above chill currents. How long would it take to die that way? Is this water cold enough to give me hypothermia? Would drowning be easier? I know it's difficult to drown one's self, that the body's will to live ensures that, given a chance, it will not succumb without a fight. I could retrace my steps to the gravel shore, scoop up enough river-rounded rocks, rocks looking from here curiously heart-shaped, place them in my pockets, then come back out to this rock, take the last stepping-stone up from its place, assuming that it can be lifted, and—holding it close to my chest—sink into the water's dark grip. If I can't lift the last stepping-stone, I could go back to Brautigan's car and get Rusty's mysterious cave-painting rock, ride it to the river's bed. I'm thinking all of these ridiculous, melodramatic things when I hear something rustling in the brush across the river to my left. Bear, I think. Shit, can bears swim?

I pull myself up out of the water slowly, as quietly as possible, fearful of attracting the attention of whatever animal—what sounds like a very large animal—skulks through the ivy, willow and pine. I catch glimpses of it, of its progress: a branch moves, a squirrel leaps suddenly treeward, an occasional bit of shaggy hide peeks between maple leaves. It moves at a relatively quick pace, not the glacial lumbering one expects from bears sniffing for honey. And it smells. That is, it reeks. Of every cologne or perfume ever devised, mixed and—on creamy white paper—stapled into a magazine's spine.

Before long, it's near the bridge where the necking couple sits parked. Although I can't see it, I can hear its movement, its struggle up the slippery slope to the road, the sliding rocks, giving dirt, snapping twigs.

When it moves out of the trees, onto the bridge, I catch myself, stop myself from yelping aloud.

This is no bear.

No bear walks upright with such grace.

No bear has arms so long, with hands so perfect, fingers so sublime.

No bear has a face so gentle, so much like an angel's, albeit one in need of a serious shave.

No bear inspires such awe or raises hackles as this creature does.

When it gets to the car, it pauses and looks in, shielding its eyes to get a better view of the backseat performance. Unlike me, it offers no excuses for its observation, tries not at all to disguise its presence. When it looks up, I see it—I swear this—I see it smile, its yellow teeth almost luminescent in the gathering gloom.

When it walks across the bridge and disappears into the brush on the other side of the river, I realize I've been holding my breath.

"Jesus Christ!" the boy screams, leaping out of the car.

The girl, clinging to his naked chest, is dragged with him. "What was that?"

"That was a Bigfoot! That was a goddamned Bigfoot!"

The boy looks around, spots me in the river below him. "Hey!" he hollers at me. "Did you see that?"

"I did!" I yell back at him.

"Fucking-A," he says, his head swiveling between me, his girlfriend and the place where the Bigfoot disappeared into the forest. "That was a fucking Bigfoot!"

"No, it was a bear," his girlfriend insists, her arms wrapped tight around him. Is it my imagination that the necklace around her neck, a necklace I couldn't possibly see from this distance, reads, in gold cursive, "DeeDee"?

"You saw it, right?" he yells at me. "You did?" Although it is impossible for me to read his license plate from this angle, I swear I can. RUSTY 1, it says. "You saw him, right?"

"I did," I say, because I did see it. And they, they saw it. And now they see me. They see me and my hook balanced shoeless on a rock in the middle of a river. They see me and they don't run, they don't scream, they don't tear off into the night, leaving a cloud of sex, panic and burning rubber. They see me and I say, "I did. I saw it."

The boy looks down at the ground in front of him. "Holy shit!" he says. He hollers at me again. "Come check this out! His fucking footprints! He left his fucking footprints all over the place! You've got to see this!"

Indeed I do. I've been invited to investigate, to see DeeDee's necklace up close, to check out Rusty's license plate, to smell their respective, liberally applied perfume and cologne. Putting on my shoes, stringing my socks on my hook's point, I move toward the first boulder bridging the river back to the shore.

I slip.

Go down hard, hitting on my back and tailbone. My head slams against the rock so violently I see double for a moment. I'm losing consciousness.

And then I'm slipping, sliding off the rock, being pulled into the river by the water, being pulled out into the current, being pulled out while my vision fades to black. Flipping onto my belly, fighting to stay awake, I begin to paddle as hard as I can, aware that I'm making no headway, but trying desperately.

And then.

My hook strikes the rock, the tabletop rock on which I'd just been sitting. And stays. Hung in a crack, stuck, sunk in like a mountaineer's pike, it holds. Slowly, beginning to cry, I pull myself up, back up onto the rock, pull myself up by my hook until the water's fingers release me, and I'm prostrate, laid out, basking in the shadows of the trees.

Not dead. Alive. Breathing hard. Heart galloping. Head throbbing. Back screaming. Hook aching. Alive. Not dead.

"Hey," the boy hollers down at me. He's halfway out of his trousers, standing bent over, apple-red boxers blowing in the wind. His girl-friend jumps up and down beside him, arms crossed in front of her brassiered chest. Her necklace is gone. "Hey," he says. "All right? Are you all right?"

"Yes," I whisper.

"You going to be okay?" he screams, standing straight, pulling his trousers back up, relieved no doubt not to be jumping in to my rescue. "Hey," he repeats, "you going to be okay?"

I don't have to think about it. I know the answer. I know what to say. I know what I'm going to say. I know what I want to say.

"Yes," I tell him, rolling over, waving my hook at him as best I can, in a way that can only be interpreted as friendly. "Yes." I pull myself up into a crouch, shake my throbbing head, clear the shadows from the corners of my vision. I stand, wave my hook at him and his girl-friend and holler, "Yes."

About the Author

A prolific short story writer and editor, Matt Clark worked for Andrei Codrescu's *Exquisite Corpse* before becoming the director of the graduate writing program at Louisiana State University at the age of twenty-nine. He died of liver and colon cancer at the age of thirty-one. *Hook Man Speaks* is his only novel.

GOV. & NEWS   COULDA MUCH WORSE
TEST INVESTED
TWO CONCERNS TRAP
— DIMINISH
— SCANDAL
—